Fenella Fang

Ritchie Perry

Illustrated by Jean Baylis

A Beaver Book

Published by Arrow Books Limited
62−65 Chandos Place, London WC2N 4NW

An imprint of Century Hutchinson Limited

London Melbourne Sydney Auckland
Johannesburg and agencies throughout
the world

First published by Hutchinson Children's Books 1986
Beaver edition 1988

Text © Ritchie Perry 1986

Illustrations © Jean Baylis 1986

Printed and bound in Great Britain by
Anchor Brendon Ltd, Tiptree, Essex.

ISBN 0 09 951270 X

One

It was pleasantly cool inside the coffin. Fenella Fang stretched and settled herself more comfortably in the damp earth. Some of her friends preferred the modern coffins with their power-assisted lids and central cooling systems. Beatrice Bite had even had a cocktail cabinet fitted in hers and said she didn't know how she had managed before. However, Fenella was old-fashioned. What had been good enough for vampires for thousands of years was good enough for her as well.

Although it was nearly dark outside, Fenella was in no great hurry to get up. She was going to visit her Uncle Samuel and she knew he would be in his coffin for some time yet. Samuel Suck, as he was called since he had lost all his teeth, was the oldest of all the vampires and since his two thousandth anniversary he had needed more and more rest. It would be bad manners for her to arrive at Blood Castle too early.

Lying there in her coffin, Fenella smiled fondly as she thought of her uncle. Some of the happiest nights of her youth had been spent playing in the dank dungeons of the old castle on the hill. It was Uncle Samuel who had given Fenella her first pet bat, Squeak. He had been with her when she had first flown on her brand-new wings, swooping down from the castle battlements to land on the forest floor beside him. Fenella promised herself that she would wear her very best shroud for the visit. Uncle Samuel might be old but there was still a twinkle in his red eyes when he saw a pretty young vampire. She also wondered what her uncle's faithful servant, Igor, would have prepared for her to eat. He always laid on something special when he knew she was coming.

It was still early but by now Fenella was too excited to stay in her coffin any longer. The lid opened with the ghastly creak that all coffin lids are supposed to have and Fenella began to sit up. She knew at once that there was something wrong. Normally she could only hear the rats scurrying across the floor or the bats squeaking in their roost near the ceiling but tonight there was a new sound. Fenella could hear muffled sobs, as though somebody was crying. When she turned her head, she could see the small shape of a girl huddled on the floor against the wall.

Quietly Fenella allowed the lid to close again and sank back into the damp earth. There was a human being in her crypt! The very thought filled Fenella with a sense of outrage. Didn't the child

know that you couldn't simply walk into somebody else's home as though it was your own? No
vampire would ever enter a human's house
without an invitation.

'Dracula's teeth,' Fenella muttered angrily to
herself. 'Why did it have to happen tonight of
all nights?'

In all the years the crypt had been her home, it
had happened only once before. Then a tramp
had found his way into the crypt and Fenella had

had to spend six long nights hiding in her coffin before the rats and bats had driven him away. Even when he had finally gone, it had taken Fenella several nights to clear up the mess he had left behind.

'It's just not good enough,' Fenella grumbled to herself. 'These humans make up terrible stories about us vampires and then they come barging into our homes without so much as a by-your-leave. Knowing my luck, the revolting little beast will have been eating garlic.'

Fenella shuddered at the thought. The merest whiff of garlic was enough to make a vampire ill for nights. And Rajeev Rip, an Indian friend of Fenella's, said there was something called curry which smelled even worse. She found this very hard to imagine.

By now it would be almost completely dark outside in the crypt and Fenella decided to risk another peep at the intruder. Very carefully she opened the lid a crack and peered out. The little girl had stopped crying now. She was sitting with her back to the wall and staring at Fenella. Her eyes were blue, not red like proper eyes should be.

'I know you're there,' the girl said in a shaky voice. 'I eat lots of carrots so I can see in the dark.'

Fenella dropped the coffin lid so suddenly, it caught her a painful blow on the head. It also started her tooth aching again. The tooth had been bothering her off and on for nights and now it began aching more than ever, a throbbing pain which seemed to fill her entire head. There was nothing worse for vampires than toothache. It was the one thing which could really hurt them and the pain did nothing to improve Fenella's temper. She had been looking forward to her night out and now it was spoiled.

'Confounded brat,' she said to herself. 'Her and her carrots, whatever they might be.'

She didn't like humans at all, apart from old Igor who had been Uncle Samuel's servant for years. Like most vampires, Fenella often had daymares about humans creeping up to her coffin while she was asleep and hammering wooden stakes through her body. This wouldn't kill her of course – nothing could kill a vampire – but it wouldn't be very pleasant to wake up with a great hunk of wood sticking out of her chest. It would ruin her shroud for a start and no vampire wanted a hole through its body. Poor old Jasper Jaws had been caught twice and now he made a strange whistling sound whenever the wind blew through the holes.

Suddenly Fenella remembered something which should have occurred to her before.

'Humans are frightened of vampires.' This was something she had never really understood. 'It's no good hiding if the little monster already knows

I'm here. I might as well scare her away.'

This time the coffin lid opened all the way and Fenella sat up properly. Her red eyes glowed like burning embers in the dark and a moonbeam made her long white teeth glisten.

'Who's there?' she demanded threateningly. 'Who has dared to disturb my sleep?'

'It's me.' The girl's voice sounded very small and frightened. 'I didn't mean to disturb you. It's just that I needed somewhere to stay.'

'Well, you can't stay here. This is my home. You do know what I am, don't you?'

'Oh yes.' The girl was trembling so much, Fenella could hear her teeth chattering. 'You're a horrible, bloodsucking vampire.'

'Exactly.'

Although Fenella thought it was most rude to call somebody horrible to their face, she was pleased to see how terrified the child was. It encouraged her to climb out of the coffin and draw herself up to her full height. When she held out her arms, the hanging folds of her shroud looked like the wings Fenella had in her bat form. Slowly and menacingly, she began to walk towards the frightened girl. As she walked, Fenella hissed between her teeth, something she thought was a very nice touch.

'Keep away from me. Don't you dare come any closer.'

The girl was holding both shaking arms out towards Fenella and she had something in her hands. It looked like two pieces of wood held in the shape of a cross. Fenella was so surprised that she stopped. It was such a strange thing to do.

'What have you got there?' she asked.

She was so surprised that she even forgot to hiss.

'It's a cross.' Although the girl's voice was still shaky, she sounded very determined. 'It frightens vampires away. While I'm holding it, you can't come any closer.'

'Don't be so silly.' Fenella really couldn't understand what the child was talking about. 'Why should I be frightened of two little pieces of wood.'

'It's a crucifix and it always works in the horror films I've seen. If I touch you with it, it will burn you and you'll scream.'

Although Fenella wasn't sure what a horror film was, she was becoming quite interested. Humans really did have the strangest ideas about vampires.

'You've got it all wrong,' she said. 'Silver would burn me a little but wood can't hurt me, no matter what shape it's in.'

'Oh.' The girl's voice was sounding very small again. 'I don't have any silver with me.'

Fenella was pleased to hear it. Also, she had just remembered that she was meant to be terrifying the girl out of her wits, not having a conversation with her.

'In that case,' she hissed, 'you'd better get away

from here. If you don't, it will be the worse for you.'.

'I don't care. I'm not going.'

The terrified girl had huddled further back against the wall but she had made no move to leave.

'Don't you realize what might happen to you if you stay?'

'Of course I know.' Now the girl was crying again. 'You're a vampire. Go on then. Do your worst and see if I care.'

To Fenella's amazement, the girl lifted her head and stretched out her neck, offering it to Fenella to bite. The very thought made the vampire shudder. She had never understood how Uncle Drac and the others had managed in the bad old nights before HBS* had been invented. The prospect of biting into some filthy, human neck made her feel quite ill. Even if she was starving, Fenella knew she could never do it. It was simply too revolting for words.

'I'll give you one last chance, child.' All the hissing was making Fenella's tooth ache more than ever. 'Run away to your home now and I won't harm you.'

'But I don't have a home to run to,' the girl wailed. 'There's nothing you can do to me that's any worse than what's been happening already.'

*Human Blood Substitute

The girl was crying in earnest now, great sobs which shook her entire body. She looked so sad and sounded so desperate that for a moment Fenella was quite touched. She almost reached out in an attempt to comfort her. Then Fenella remembered who she was and what she was supposed to be doing.

'Listen to me,' she hissed. 'I don't mind where you go but you're not staying here. I have to go out and I don't want you to be here when I return. If you are, I'll show you just how horrible a blood-sucking vampire can be.'

With this, Fenella turned on her heel and stalked back to her coffin.

'That's shown her,' she thought. 'That will teach her to mess with me.'

But there was no real satisfaction in the thought. Frightening the child had simply made her feel mean. Fenella felt like a bully and, worse still, deep down she was beginning to be sorry for the child. It was almost as though her toothache was a punishment for the way she had behaved.

After a while the girl's sobbing stopped. Apart from the odd sniff, she was quiet but it still wasn't easy not to cry.

'Stop feeling sorry for yourself,' she told herself fiercely as the tears welled into her eyes again. 'Things could be much worse.'

The trouble was, she couldn't think how

because it had been the longest, most miserable and most frightening day of her entire life. It had got off to a terrible start when she discovered that Spot had gone. Spot was her puppy. He had been a present from her father before he left to work in Nigeria and the little Dalmation had soon become her best friend. Whenever she had felt lonely or unhappy, she had only had to cuddle him to feel better at once. And now he was gone for ever.

'He's far too vicious to keep,' her cousin Fred had said with his great, stupid grin. 'He's dangerous. Why, he might bite you or something.'

'Spot would never do that.'

'Well he bit me, didn't he?'

Fred had held up his bandaged hand as proof.

'That was your own silly fault. You shouldn't have tormented him so. What did you expect Spot to do when you kept pinching his ears and pulling his tail?'

This was something she had tried to explain to her aunt and uncle but it had been no use. Although they had been very kind to her, they always took Fred's side in any argument. He was their only child and in their eyes he was perfect. They simply couldn't believe their son would ever lie to them.

The girl knew different. She knew that her cousin was the meanest, most horrible boy in the whole world. Ever since she had gone to stay with her aunt and uncle at the fair, Fred had done his best to make her life a misery. The very thought of some of the things he had done to her brought the tears back to her eyes.

With Spot gone, there was nobody to comfort her and she had decided to run away. She had had no real idea where she was going. All she knew was that she must find somewhere else to stay until her father returned. The preparations had been simple. She had simply put some tins of food and a change of clothes into a bag and off she had gone.

She had walked all day long, following the signs which pointed towards London. This was where she had lived with Dad before he had gone to work in Nigeria and her whole life had been turned upside down. Unfortunately, she hadn't realized quite how far it was. Although she had walked and walked until her legs ached, London was still well over a hundred miles away when it started to get dark.

At first she hadn't been sure what to do. She knew she needed somewhere to spend the night but she didn't have any money and she couldn't simply knock at a door and ask for a room. Dad had always told her not to talk to strangers. This was why she hadn't tried to thumb a lift in any of the cars which had gone flashing past her while she had been walking.

What Dad hadn't told her about was vampires. When she had found the crypt near the ruined church in the middle of the old graveyard she had thought this would be the perfect place to spend the night. She would be out of the wind and she was sure nobody would disturb her. The thought of being in a graveyard didn't worry her at all. She was a sensible little girl and she didn't believe in ghosts.

Come to that, she hadn't believed in vampires either until the coffin lid opened and the hideous creature had emerged. It had been terrible and for a moment she was sure that her heart had stopped beating. Later, when the monster had left the coffin and started coming towards her, it had been even worse. The sight of those long, sharp teeth and glowing eyes had started her shaking like a jelly. She was sure her last moment had come and she would have run, but her legs would not work.

However, the longer the vampire had talked, the less frightened she had become. Despite all the horrible threats the creature was making, she had sensed that it didn't really mean her any harm. Although the vampire looked hideous, she was already becoming used to her. Dad had always told her not to judge people by their appearance.

'Besides, she doesn't really look much worse than cousin Fred,' the girl said to herself. 'He looks pretty terrible with those zits all over his face and his runny nose. He could probably play Frankenstein without needing any make-up.'

Now the vampire had stopped threatening her, the girl had become quite interested in what the creature was doing. She had always been able to see well in the dark and she watched in fascination as Fenella prepared to go out. Although it looked like an ordinary coffin which the vampire had been using, it obviously wasn't. When the vampire touched the front of it, a drawer shot out. The long, black shroud Fenella took out fell almost to her feet when she put it on. After she had closed the drawer, the vampire touched another part of the coffin and a small dressing table appeared, complete with vanity mirror and make-up.

The girl was so intrigued her fears were completely forgotten. Quietly she rose to her feet and tiptoed across the crypt to stand behind Fenella. She had never seen a vampire getting ready for a night out before.

Fenella rubbed the powder into her cheeks until they had just the greenish tinge which Uncle Samuel liked. Next came the lipstick and she put it on carefully until her lips were a glistening blood-red. Looking at her reflection in the mirror, Fenella knew that she had seldom looked more beautiful, not even on that never-to-be-

forgotten night when she was voted Miss Vampire of the Year. To look at her, nobody would realize how much she was suffering from toothache.

'It's a wonderful coffin,' the girl said.

'It is, isn't it?'

Fenella hadn't heard the girl come up behind her but she was pleased with the remark. She was very proud of her coffin. It had been given to her on her hundredth anniversary, when Fenella had come of age, and it had been made by the best craftsmen in Transylvania.

'How do all the drawers and things fit in? Don't they poke into you when you're inside?'

This made Fenella laugh. To a human it was a hideous sound, rather like a pig being strangled. The girl flinched back, thinking the vampire must be angry with her, but Fenella didn't notice.

'Of course not, silly,' she said. 'It's a special vampire coffin. It's much bigger than it seems.'

'Like the Tardis, you mean.'

'What's a Tardis?'

The girl didn't have a chance to explain about Dr Who because she had suddenly noticed something. Although Fenella was looking into the mirror while she applied her make-up, there was no reflection. The girl couldn't see the vampire's face in the mirror at all.

'There's nothing there,' she said.

'What do you mean, child?' Fenella had no idea what she was talking about.

'Your face doesn't show up in the mirror.'

'Of course it does. It's there.'

The vampire used one claw-like finger to point at her reflection.

'I can't see anything. The mirror looks empty to me.'

'It must be because you're human.' Fenella had just remembered something she had been told a long time ago. 'Humans never can see vampires' reflections in mirrors. I can though.'

'Oh.'

The girl clearly didn't understand and Fenella wasn't entirely sure she did either. All she knew was that it had something to do with vampires being neither dead nor alive.

Puckering her lips at herself in the mirror, Fenella decided that she looked superb. There was just one final thing to do. Unstoppering a small bottle, she dabbed a couple of drops of liquid behind each of her pointed ears.

'Ugh!' The girl sounded as though she was going to be sick. 'What's that horrible smell?'

'Don't be so rude.'

Fenella was quite upset. It was Eau de Rot, her very favourite perfume. Besides, she had just realized that she was doing it again, talking to the child as though she was a friend, not some nuisance who had come barging into her home. Fenella swung round with a snarl and the girl rapidly stepped back.

'Just remember what I told you, child,' Fenella hissed, her eyes glowing. 'I don't want to find you here when I come back.'

Then, in front of the girl's eyes, Fenella rose to her feet and changed into her bat form. Her arms were transformed into great, black wings. Her hands and feet became claws and black fur covered her face. Only her teeth and her eyes remained the same. With one last glare at the girl, Fenella flapped her wings and soared up into the air, leaving the crypt through a hole in the ceiling.

Open-mouthed with amazement, the girl watched her go, staring upwards until long after the vampire had disappeared into the night sky.

Two

Igor's father had been an Igor too and so had his grandfather. In fact, all the menfolk in his family had been called Igor for as far back as anybody could remember. His ancestors had been working at Blood Castle for centuries and it made things much easier for old Samuel Suck if they all had the same name. Besides, Samuel enjoyed shouting out 'Igor' whenever he wanted anything. It was his favourite name and there was a nice ring to it as it bounced back off the damp, slime-covered walls.

Unfortunately, Igor knew he would be the very last of his line. He had no son to carry on the family tradition. Although Igor would have liked to be married and have children of his own, he had never met a woman who wanted to be his wife. There weren't many women who had any desire to live with somebody who never washed or changed his clothes, who ate raw meat and whose favourite hobby was pulling the wings off flies.

In any case, Igor was ugly. To be honest, he was

very, very ugly indeed, quite possibly the ugliest man in the whole, wide world. Most people would be more frightened by Igor's appearance than they would be by Samuel Suck's or Fenella's. Igor was so ugly that when he left the castle to go shopping, all the people in the village at the foot of the hill would put on blindfolds so they didn't have to see him. Not that Igor minded this too much. It meant he could go into the village shop, fill his sack with all manner of good things and then only pay for a penny stick of liquorice. As nobody dared look at him, nobody knew what he was stealing.

Those poor people who did see Igor usually had nightmares for months afterwards because he was truly horrible. For a start, his arms and legs were all different sizes, as though they had been intended for several different people. When he walked, Igor always looked as though he was going uphill round a corner.

His huge head was completely bald and covered with warts except in those places where a greenish mould grew. Worse still, his face looked as though it had once been stamped on by a giant foot, with everything squashed into the wrong place. His eyes, nose and mouth were all squeezed to one side of his face while on the other there was nothing except warts, mould and a single ear which would have made an elephant proud.

Nor was this all. Igor's nose dripped all the time, like a tap whose washer had gone wrong, and his mouth was filled with filthy, rotting teeth. Although he was bald, Igor still suffered from terrible dandruff, making the warts on top of his head look like miniature ice-capped mountains. If he ever shook his head, his face would be hidden by a snowstorm of dandruff. As his face was so hideous, this was probably a good thing. And finally, of course, there was Igor's smell, the odour of somebody who had never used a bar of soap in his life. It was so bad that most people tried not to breathe too much while they were in his company.

However ugly Igor might seem to other humans, Fenella loved him almost as much as her uncle. As soon as she had landed on the castle battlements and changed back into her normal form, she threw her arms around him and nuzzled his neck. Vampires never kissed because their teeth got in the way.

'It's good to see you, Igor,' she said affectionately. 'You're better-looking every time I see you.'

'Thank you, Miss Fenella,' Igor mumbled. When he blushed, all his warts glowed blood-red.

'Where's Uncle Samuel?'

'He's still in his coffin, Miss. He seems to be sleeping later and later nowanights.'

'Come on then, Igor. Let's go and wake him up.'

Fenella was almost prancing as she started down the stairs and Igor found it difficult to keep up with her. It was all right going up the spiral staircase but when he went down, his short leg was on the wrong side. This meant he bumped into the walls a lot.

Uncle Samuel's coffin stood on a platform in the castle's largest dungeon. Fenella had always thought it was one of the nicest rooms she had ever seen. Rusty chains and thumbscrews hung on the stone walls. Other old instruments of torture were scattered about the place, all of them festooned with cobwebs, and there were no windows to allow in any light. As the dungeon was below ground, it was always delightfully cool, even on the hottest summer day. It was the ideal place for a vampire to live.

Fenella ran up the stone steps to stand beside the coffin. From inside she could hear the little bubbling snores her uncle was making as he slept. With a smile at Igor, she raised her hand and knocked on the lid.

'Wakey, wakey, Uncle,' she called. 'It's time to get up.'

The snoring continued. By now Igor was standing beside her and he shook his head, showering her with white flakes.

'You won't wake the Master like that, Miss. I

have to use this now. Your uncle is becoming very hard of hearing.'

The servant had an ear trumpet in his hand. He gave it to Fenella to hold while he lifted the coffin lid. Samuel Suck was sleeping as peacefully as only a two thousand three hundred and twenty-one year old vampire could. His mouth hung open, exposing his toothless gums, and there was a smile on his lips as though his dream was a happy one.

'Dear old thing,' Fenella said, smiling to herself as she leaned forward to pat his scaly forehead.

'If you move out of the way, Miss, I'll have him up in a jiffy.'

Igor held the thin end of the trumpet against Samuel's ear. Then he took a deep breath and shouted into the other end as loudly as he could.

'WAKE UP, MASTER. RISE AND SHINE.'

The very walls of the dungeon seemed to shake but Samuel's eyelids only flickered once before he continued snoring. Igor took an even deeper breath before he tried again.

'COME ON, YOU OLD BAT,' he bellowed. 'MISS FENELLA IS HERE.'

This time Samuel Suck's eyes shot wide open and he sat up in the coffin.

'There's no need to shout, Igor,' he said sternly. 'I was awake already.'

'Yes, Master. I'm sorry, Master.'

26

Igor winked at Fenella, making himself look more hideous than usual, and she tried very hard not to smile – without much success.

'It's nice to see you, Fenella,' Samuel continued. 'I must say I like that shroud you're wearing. Is it new?'

'Yes, Uncle. I made it myself.'

'You always were a clever little thing. Why don't you go upstairs with young Igor while I get myself dressed? I shan't be a moment.'

Once the other two had left the dungeon, Samuel climbed out of his coffin and started pulling open drawers. He was looking for his best cloak, the one with the red silk lining. Old Samuel always liked to dress up when his favourite niece came visiting.

'Is something the matter, Miss?'

Igor was concerned. He had prepared the toad-liver pasties especially because he knew they were Fenella's favourites. However, she had only taken one small bite before she returned the pasty to her plate.

'It's nothing, Igor,' Fenella said bravely. 'Just a spot of toothache.'

By now the pain was worse than ever.

'Oh dear, Miss.' Although Fenella tried to make light of it, Igor was more concerned than ever. He knew there was nothing worse for a vampire than a bad toothache. Sometimes it could even stop them flying. The pain spoiled their sense of direction and they flew into trees and things. 'Have you had it long?'

'Only for the last few days.'

Fenella gently touched the aching tooth with the tip of her tongue but this was a mistake. It hurt so much she felt as though her whole head was being torn apart. Igor noticed at once.

'It looks bad, Miss. It would be best to take it out.'

'I will, Igor, just as soon as it's loose.'

'There's no need to wait Miss – I could do it for you now. I like pulling out teeth.'

He enjoyed pulling out teeth almost as much as he enjoyed tearing the wings off flies and butterflies.

'That's very kind of you, Igor.' Fenella sounded doubtful. 'All the same, it might be better to leave the tooth for a while.'

'I always used to do your uncle's teeth for him, Miss.'

'I didn't know that.'

'Oh yes, Miss. The Master used to swear by me.'

Another searing pain in her jaw made up Fenella's mind for her. The tooth really was hurting very badly and what had been good enough for Uncle Samuel was surely good enough for her.

'You're sure you know how to do it properly?' she asked.

'Oh yes, Miss.'

'In that case I'd be most grateful to you.'

'That's very sensible, Miss. You just wait here. I shan't be a moment.'

The servant scuttled out of the room, leering all over his horrible face. A minute later he returned. He was carrying a rusty old pair of pliers, a hammer and a chisel. Fenella could understand what the pliers were for but she wasn't so sure about the other tools.

'What do you need them for?' she enquired.

'Sometimes the tooth breaks, Miss,' he explained. 'Then I have to chisel the roots out of the gum. But don't worry your pretty little head about it – you'll hardly feel a thing.'

By now Fenella was beginning to suspect that it might be better to have toothache than to let Igor loose in her mouth with a hammer and chisel. Unfortunately, it was too late for her to change her mind. Igor had already pulled her mouth open and was peering excitedly inside. Most humans would have been terrified to be so close to a vampire's teeth. However, Igor had been working with vampires all his life.

'Ah, there it is, Miss,' he said. 'It will all be over in a jiffy.'

The pliers and one of Igor's wartcovered hands were inside Fenella's mouth. He was drooling with pleasure.

'IGOR!' The sound of Samuel Suck's voice

filled the hall of the castle like a clap of thunder. 'WHAT DO YOU THINK YOU'RE DOING?'

Igor jumped back as though he had been bitten. In fact, he very nearly was because Fenella was so startled that her teeth closed together with a snap.

'It's all right, Uncle. I have a bad tooth and Igor is going to pull it out for me.'

'I'd have thought you had more sense than that, Fenella.' Uncle Samuel looked astounded.

'But Igor told me he looked after your teeth for you.' Fenella couldn't understand why her uncle was so upset. 'He said you swore by him.'

'Swore *at* him, more like.' Samuel snorted in disgust. 'How do you think I lost all my lovely teeth?'

'I thought they all fell out, Uncle.'

'Fell out, my foot. It was all Igor's fault. I had terrible toothache once and I was fool enough to let him help. He pulled out every tooth in my head before he finally found the one which was bad.'

'It was a mistake anybody could have made, Master.' Igor was grovelling at Samuel's feet. 'It won't happen again.'

'Too right it won't,' Samuel told him. 'If you so much as mention the word tooth in my presence again, I shall banish you from the castle for ever.'

'Please don't do that, Master.'

Igor crawled across the floor and was kissing his Master's feet until Samuel kicked him away. Fenella simply sank back in her seat and clutched her aching jaw. She knew she had had a very narrow escape.

Old Samuel Suck wasn't simply famous for not having any teeth. He was also one of the greatest of all vampire inventors. Way back in the dark mists of time, when Samuel was still only in his hundreds, he had helped in the work on the most important discovery in the history of vampiredom, HBS*. Since then he had been responsible for many other inventions. The Coffin Safety Hinge (COSH for short) had been entirely his work. He had realized it was necessary after Nathaniel Nibble, a friend of his, had been trapped for three months when the lid had fallen on him while he was halfway out of his coffin. Countless other vampires had encountered similar trouble but the problem had disappeared thanks to Samuel's new hinge. Once the hinge had been fitted, it became impossible for a coffin lid to fall by accident. The invention had been so successful that *The Vampire Nightly* had devoted two whole pages to Samuel's achievement.

Of course, not all his inventions had been quite so successful. Quite recently, for example, Samuel had become concerned with the problems vampires faced when they were flying on moonless

*Human Blood Substitute

nights. Unless they had toothache, vampires were like bats and never bumped into anything. However, it wasn't at all unusual for other night creatures to fly into vampires simply because they didn't see them coming. Even for a fully-grown vampire, it wasn't at all pleasant to have an owl fly straight into you. There had been nothing wrong with Samuel's idea of fitting small lights to the tips of vampires' wings. Unfortunately, it wasn't just owls who noticed the lights. Before long the human newspapers were full of stories about UFOs while the vampires were soon fed up with fighter planes buzzing around them every time they went out for a flight.

Over breakfast, Samuel explained his latest idea to Fenella. In all their long history, vampires had never been able to go out in daylight. Not only was the sun bad for vampires' skins but any bright light could damage their sensitive eyes. This wasn't too bad in winter, when night came early, but in summer vampires might have to spend as much as eighteen hours every day in their coffins. Now Samuel had found a solution to the age-old problem. He had prepared a special ointment which would keep the skin dry and scaly and a pair of goggles which would protect the eyes from even the brightest light.

'Just think of it, Fenella,' he cried. 'A whole new world will be open to us vampires. We'll be able to go out whenever we feel like it. If we suffer from insomnia, we won't have to toss and turn in our coffins until it's dark. It won't matter if we stay out late at a party. I'm sure it's going to be the most important of all my inventions.'

'That's nice, Uncle.'

Although Fenella had tried to pay attention, she had too much on her mind to be really enthusiastic. It wasn't simply the toothache which was bothering her. She couldn't help remembering the girl she had left behind in the crypt.

'It's already been tested,' Samuel went on, 'and it works perfectly. I'd try it out myself if I could stay awake long enough.'

'That's nice, Uncle.'

This time Samuel realized there was something wrong. He stopped talking about his invention and peered across the table at Fenella.

'What's the matter?' he asked. 'Is that tooth of yours still playing you up?'

'I wish that was all, Uncle,' Fenella wailed. 'It's far worse than that.'

It didn't take her very long to explain about the unwelcome visitor to the crypt. Both Samuel and Igor were appalled by what they heard. They knew that this was almost the worst disaster which could befall a vampire.

'I just don't know what to do, Uncle,' Fenella finished. 'Do you have any ideas?'

For several seconds old Samuel remained silent, his head bowed in thought. Then he looked up at Fenella.

'There's only one thing you can do,' he said. 'It's unpleasant but I can't see any alternative.'

'That's right, Master.' There was a grotesque leer on Igor's hideous face. 'We'll have to kill the interfering little busybody. That'll shut her up all right.'

Fenella and her uncle turned to look at the servant in surprise.

'I'll do it for you, Miss,' Igor continued eagerly, beginning to drool again. 'I'll slit her throat and hang her upside down so all the blood drains out. Then I'll tear off her arms and legs and put them through my mincer. After that I could ... OUCH!'

Igor yelped with pain as Samuel leaned out of his chair to cuff him around the ears.

'Stop it at once, Igor,' he said sternly. 'You ought to know me better than that by now. That wasn't what I was going to suggest at all.'

'What did you have in mind?' Fenella asked.

'Well, dear, I hate to say it but you'll have to leave your crypt and move somewhere else.'

'That's what I was afraid you'd say.'

Fenella was gloomier than ever.

'As I said, you don't have any choice. If the child has already seen you, she's bound to tell somebody else. You know what humans are like. Once they know where you are, you'll never have a moment's peace.'

'I suppose you're right,' Fenella sighed. 'The

trouble is, I'm so fond of my crypt. I'm sure I won't be able to find anywhere else that's quite so cosy.'

'Try and look on the dark side, Fenella,' her uncle told her. 'You can come and stay here with me while you're sorting yourself out. I'll get Igor to make sure the earth in the spare coffin is nice and damp.'

'I still think my idea was better,' Igor muttered under his breath.

But he made sure neither Fenella nor Samuel heard him. He knew better than to make his Master angry with him.

Three

Fenella wasn't particularly surprised to discover that her uninvited guest was still in the crypt. The girl was sitting against the same patch of wall and her blue eyes were wide open. She had obviously been waiting for Fenella to return.

'You're still here, then.'

'It's like I told you,' the little girl said. 'I don't have anywhere else to go.'

'Aren't you frightened of what I might do to you?' Fenella asked.

She knew all the silly stories humans told their children about vampires.

'I'm terrified.' There was a tremble in the girl's voice. 'All the time you've been gone, I've been trying to convince myself that you won't really hurt me.'

'What makes you think that?'

'Well, if you were going to do anything horrible to me, you would have done it when you first found me. You try to sound fierce and nasty but I don't think you're really like that. Underneath, you're probably quite nice. At least, I hope you are.'

For a moment Fenella was too amazed to speak. The girl wasn't at all like the humans she had been told about. However much of a nuisance she might be, she sounded a sensible little thing. Under different circumstances, Fenella could almost imagine herself liking the child.

'You're right,' she said. 'I won't do anything to hurt you so you needn't worry. In fact, you're welcome to stay here as long as you like.'

Fenella walked over to the coffin and began opening the drawers one by one, stacking the contents on the lid. She might be forced to leave her lovely crypt but all her possessions would be going with her. Later on she would send a hearse to collect the coffin. She was sure Igor could arrange this for her.

For a while the girl watched her work in silence. Then she could contain her curiosity no longer.

'What are you doing?' she asked.

'I would have thought that was obvious.' No matter how hard she tried, Fenella couldn't keep the sadness out of her voice. 'I shall be leaving the crypt tomorrow night. I'd go now if it wasn't so late.'

'But why? This is your home.'

'It was my home,' Fenella corrected her. 'Thanks to you, I can't stay here any longer.'

When she heard Fenella say this, the girl rose to her feet and bent down to pick up the bag beside her. With one last look at the vampire, she started towards the door.

'Now what are you doing, child?' Fenella demanded.

'It's your home,' the girl said, 'so I'm the one who ought to leave. I didn't realize I was upsetting you so much. All I wanted was a place to stay for a few days.'

She sounded very small and alone. The child was so obviously unhappy that, despite her own problems, Fenella was beginning to feel sorry for her. It wasn't right that anyone so young should be all on her own.

'I've already told you that you can stay,' she said in a more kindly fashion. 'The damage is done now. I shall have to leave whether you go or not.'

'I don't understand.' The girl was clearly bewildered. 'If I'm such a problem, why haven't you killed me.'

'Vampires don't kill humans,' Fenella explained. 'Only other humans do that. Besides, it's not really you who's the problem. I'm worried about the other humans you'll speak to. Once other people know I'm here, they won't rest until they drive me away. That's why I'm going tomorrow, before they have the chance.'

'I wouldn't tell anybody else about you if you didn't want me to.' The girl sounded indignant. 'I wouldn't want to get you into trouble.'

'That's easy to say now, but sooner or later

you'll change your mind. You'll want to tell some-body else about the vampire you met.'

'But I won't. I promise I won't tell another living soul. Dad says I'm better at keeping a secret than anybody he's ever met.'

The girl sounded as though she was speaking the truth and Fenella would have liked to have believed her. Unfortunately, all vampires knew it was never safe to trust a human. When her packing was done and Fenella finally climbed into her coffin, she was still determined to leave the crypt the following night.

During the day Fenella's toothache became much worse. In fact, it was hurting her so much that she was unable to sleep and she spent most of the daylight hours tossing or turning in her coffin. Once or twice she was tempted to get up and make an early start to the night. Uncle Samuel had made her a present of a tube of his new ointment and a pair of goggles before she left Blood Castle. Now would have been a good time to test them out if Fenella hadn't been certain her tooth would hurt just as much whether she was in her coffin or out of it.

By evening the pain was so agonizing that Fenella knew she would find it difficult to walk, let alone fly. She knew her departure for Blood Castle would have to be postponed. When she climbed out of her coffin, it did nothing to improve her temper to see the girl still sitting against the wall.

'Hello, vampire.'

Fenella simply snorted in reply and pressed the button to bring out her dressing table. A quick glance in the mirror confirmed her worst fears. One side of her face was swollen to twice its normal size.

'Dracula's teeth,' she muttered. 'I should have let Igor carry on last night. Nothing could be worse than this.'

The entire side of her face was throbbing, making it difficult for her to think straight. When she gingerly touched the bad tooth with her tongue, the pain became almost unbearable. It was as though a red-hot nail had been driven into her jaw and Fenella groaned out loud.

'Is something the matter?' the girl asked anxiously.

'Of course not. I always groan when I'm having fun.'

'Your face is all swollen,' the girl went on. 'You look ever so strange.'

'You'll look strange too if you don't stop making personal remarks,' Fenella snapped bad-temperedly.

For a moment or two the girl was silent. She had had toothache herself so she knew just how bad it could be. There was no way for her to know that it was much, much worse for a vampire.

'You ought to go to a dentist,' she said at last.

'What's a dentist?'

This was a word Fenella had never heard before.

'Dentists look after your teeth and stop them hurting. If a tooth is really bad, they take it out for you. They're ever so good.'

'I suppose they use hammers and chisels.'

Fenella was remembering Igor.

'Of course they don't. They have special instruments and it doesn't hurt at all.'

'You're lucky, then. We vampires don't have dentists.'

Although she was too polite to say so, the girl thought this was rather stupid. With all the teeth they had, dentists were just what vampires needed. She only had to look at Fenella to see how much she was suffering.

It was while she was looking at Fenella that the idea suddenly came to the girl. Although the vampire was very tall compared with a human woman, this wouldn't matter too much. She could pretend to be a basketball player or something. The glowing eyes and the greenish skin were more of a problem but they could always be covered over. There wasn't much she could do about Fenella's strange smell but lots of humans smelled strange too.

'I've had an idea,' she said.

42

'What do you want me to do? Cheer?'

If anything, the tooth was hurting more than ever. However, Fenella's bad temper didn't put the girl off.

'As vampires don't have dentists,' she went on, 'you could go to a human dentist.'

'That's really brilliant, child,' Fenella said sarcastically. 'I'm sure nobody would notice a vampire walking down the street. I haven't heard such a stupid suggestion for centuries.'

'There's no need to be nasty. I was only trying to help.'

Suddenly, Fenella felt ashamed of herself. It wasn't the girl's fault that she was in such agony.

'I'm sorry,' she said, 'but it really wouldn't work. Vampires can't mix with humans.'

'That's the whole point – nobody would know you were a vampire. We could easily disguise you so you looked just like a human.'

This was a thought which didn't please Fenella at all. She had always considered humans to be rather ugly creatures.

'It still wouldn't work, I'm afraid. I don't know anything about human customs. I could never manage to pass myself off as one of them.'

'You'd have me to help you.'

'You mean you'd go with me?'

The girl nodded and once again Fenella found herself thinking how unusual she was for a human. She seemed so eager to help, there were moments when Fenella almost liked her. It was unfortunate that her idea was simply too ridiculous for words. Fenella knew she could never force herself to go into a human town while all the people were awake.

Or could she? Another searing pain from the infected tooth brought the tears springing into Fenella's eyes. Surely almost anything would be better than this.

'Do you really think I could pass as a human?' she asked.

'I'm sure of it,' the girl told her. 'Just think – one quick visit to the nearest dentist and you wouldn't have toothache any more.'

Perhaps it could be done. Humans couldn't harm her even if she was recognized as a vampire so there wasn't anything for her to worry about. It might be worth the risk simply to be rid of the pain which was driving her mad.

'You say you'll come with me?' she asked the girl.

'I'll stay with you all the time. I can help you disguise yourself as well.'

'All right.' Fenella took a deep breath before she uttered the fateful words. 'Let's try it.'

'It's the sensible thing to do,' the girl told her. 'We can go first thing in the morning—'

And then she stopped because something had just occurred to her. Something which would ruin her entire plan.

'Oh dear,' she said in a sad voice. 'I've just remembered. Vampires can't go out in daylight and dentists don't work at night.'

For a moment, Fenella's spirits drooped too until she realized that thanks to Uncle Samuel's marvellous ointment, daylight was no longer a problem for her. Once she had explained this to the child, the two of them made their plans for the morning. By the time they had finished, Fenella was feeling much better disposed towards the girl. She definitely wasn't at all bad for a human.

'I think it's about time we introduced ourselves,' she said. 'My name is Fenella. What's yours?'

'It's—' the girl began. Then she hesitated and shook her head. 'No, I'd better not tell you. If you know who I am, you might try to send me back where I came from.'

No matter how hard Fenella tried to persuade her, the girl wouldn't change her mind. Later on, however, just before morning when the girl had finally fallen into an exhausted sleep, Fenella crept across the crypt and took a look inside her bag. It didn't take the vampire long to find what she wanted because the girl's name was written all over several of the possessions inside. HEINZ BEANS might be a strange name but, as Fenella knew, human beings were very strange creatures.

Petunia Pringle was short-sighted, so short-sighted in fact that she had to wear a pair of special glasses which made her look rather like an owl. The first she knew about Fenella's arrival was the smell. It resembled the smell she had when her drains were blocked at home. Petunia wasn't to know that it was produced by Samuel Suck's ointment, which he had perfumed especially for his favourite niece. The girl thought it was far worse than Eau de Rot although Fenella had been delighted.

'Yes, Madam,' Petunia began. 'Can I—'

She stopped suddenly in mid-sentence with her mouth hanging open. Even through her thick, pebble lenses, she could see there was something very unusual indeed about the lady who had just come through the door. She was huge, almost a giantess, and she towered over Petunia who was sitting at her desk. And her clothes! Petunia had never seen anything like them. A tattered old shawl covered the top of her head and was wrapped around the lower part of her face. Most of the rest of her face was covered by an enormous pair of goggles.

Perhaps she's a welder, Petunia thought to herself. Either that or she's just been skiing. But that dress of hers. It's covered with little bits of earth. It looks as though she took it from somebody in a coffin.

However, Petunia was a kindly soul and the woman was obviously in pain. One side of her face was badly swollen beneath the shawl and what little skin she could see was a shiny, greenish colour.

'Yes, Madam,' Petunia said again, trying not to breathe too deeply as the smell was making her feel ill. 'Can I help you?'

'I hope so.' Although the woman's voice was muffled by the shawl, there was something about it that sent a shiver down Petunia's spine. 'I've got toothache.'

'I see. Are you a regular patient of Mr Pullit's?'

The woman looked as though she didn't understand the question but the girl with her answered for her.

'It's the first time she's been here,' she explained. 'It's an emergency.'

Petunia looked in the appointment book. Although it was full for the entire morning, she never turned anybody away who was in real pain.

'Mr Pullit is very busy today,' she said, 'but he'll see you later if you go through to the waiting room. First of all, though, I'd better have a few details.

She pulled a card towards her and picked up a pen.

'What's your name, please?' she asked.

'Fenella,' Fenella answered.

'Are you a Mrs?'

'I'm a Fang.'

As vampires didn't marry, Fenella didn't have the slightest idea what the woman was talking about.

'It's Miss Fenella Fang,' the girl interrupted quickly.

Petunia carefully wrote the name down. She was beginning to think that it might not be a bad idea if the woman was locked away for her own safety. Not only did she look and smell strange, she behaved as though she had lost her marbles.

'Address?'

'No, it's a shroud actually.' Fenella was pleased that Petunia had noticed. 'I made it myself.'

'She means The Crypt, Cemetery Lane,' the girl said quickly, kicking Fenella on the ankle.

'Age?'

'Three hundred and—'

There was no chance for Fenella to finish because she had just been kicked on the ankle again.

'She's twenty-seven,' the girl answered.

'Fine. And what's your date of birth?'

'The 43rd of Bladderwort, 3098.'

As she had no way of knowing that vampires had a completely different calendar from humans, this was where Petunia decided to give up. The little girl seemed normal enough but the woman was definitely crazy. All Petunia could hope was that she wasn't violent.

'Perhaps you'd like to go through into the waiting room Miss Fang,' she said weakly. 'Mr Pullit will see you as soon as he can.'

By now Petunia was sure that this wasn't going to be her day.

Mr Pullit was a very good dentist and the waiting room was full of patients. There was only one chair left in the corner and Fenella sat on it while the girl stood beside her.

'Just look at all the people,' she said. 'We'll probably have to wait for hours.'

'Never mind,' Fenella answered. 'It will be worth it if this dentist of yours can do something about my tooth.'

It was rather stuffy in the room and Fenella was beginning to feel uncomfortably warm. She was used to a nice, cool crypt, not heated waiting rooms. The shawl was irritating her, especially where it touched her swollen cheek, and without thinking Fenella pulled it away from the lower part of her face. All the adults were too busy reading their magazines to notice but Francis Frump was too young to read. He had been watching Fenella even before she removed the shawl.

'Mum,' he whispered. 'Look at the funny woman sitting in the corner.'

'Shh, Francis,' Mrs Frump said without raising her head. 'It's bad manners to stare.'

'But she's ever so strange, Mum.' Francis spoke louder this time. 'She's got green skin.'

This time Mrs Frump did stop reading to peer at Fenella over the top of her magazine. She could see at once that Francis was right – the woman in the corner was very strange indeed. Her skin could have been that greenish colour because she was ill but the woman was so tall and wearing such outlandish clothes that she made Mrs Frump feel uneasy. She could have sworn the woman's eyes were glowing behind those ridiculous goggles.

Several of the other patients were also staring at Fenella by now and they felt just the same as Mrs

Frump. They were uneasy without really knowing why.

'Look at her fingers, Mum.' Francis was excited by now and everybody in the waiting room could hear him. 'They're like great claws.'

Everybody was looking at Fenella and the girl was beginning to feel most uncomfortable. However, she wasn't quite sure what to do. Perhaps it hadn't been such a good idea to bring Fenella to the dentist after all.

The only one in the waiting room who was

unaware of all the fuss was Fenella herself. In fact, she was so tired she kept nodding off. Walking took so much more energy than flying and by this time in the morning she should have been fast asleep in her coffin. Thinking of sleep made Fenella want to yawn. For a moment or two she fought to hold it back but it was no good. She was going to yawn and that was all there was to it.

None of the other patients could believe their eyes when Fenella's mouth opened in a yawn. They had never, ever seen teeth like the ones which were revealed – very few humans had – and the sight chilled them to the marrow. A few of those sitting nearest to Fenella started trembling uncontrollably, but it was Mrs Frump who acted first.

'Come on, Francis,' she said, rising hastily to her feet. 'I've just remembered that I left the gas on.'

'But we don't have gas, Mum.'

Mrs Frump ignored her son and continued towards the door, dragging Francis along behind her. At almost the same moment, all the other people in the waiting room remembered that they had left taps running or fires burning or were worried that their parrots might be about to have puppies. Whatever the reason, they had all decided they urgently needed to be somewhere else, somewhere a long way away from those terr-ible teeth, and for a few seconds they were jammed in the doorway as they fought to escape. In less than a minute, the waiting room was completely empty apart from Fenella and the girl.

Fenella had dozed off and it was the sound of the street door banging shut behind the last of the frightened patients which jerked her eyes open again. She was astonished to find herself and the girl alone. In fact, she bent down to look under the chairs in case the other patients were hiding.

'Where is everybody?' she asked.

'They've all gone,' the girl told her. 'They were scared.'

'Oh dear. This dentist of yours can't be very good if he frightens away his own patients.'

There was no opportunity for the child to answer because at this moment Petunia Pringle came bustling into the waiting room.

'Mr Sanderson,' she cooed sweetly as she came in through the door. 'Mr Pullit will see you now.'

Then Petunia stopped because she could see that Mr Sanderson wasn't there. Nor were Miss Pomfret, Colonel Bogey or the Whalebellies. In fact, all the patients she had seen come in earlier had gone and Petunia couldn't understand this at all. Taking off her glasses and polishing them didn't make any difference. The waiting room was empty apart from that weird Miss Fang and the girl.

'Where have they all gone?' she asked weakly.

'They remembered they had urgent appointments somewhere else,' the girl answered quickly, not allowing Fenella a chance to speak.

'All of them?'

'All of them,' the girl said firmly.

'In that case, you'd better come through, Miss Fang. It appears that Mr Pullit can see you much sooner than I expected.'

Petunia still thought it was most odd but there was nothing at all she could do about it.

Four

After Petunia had shown Fenella and the girl into the surgery, she left them there on their own, saying Mr Pullit would be with them in a minute. By now Fenella was beginning to feel rather nervous. She had met more humans in the past hour or so than she had in the previous three hundred and twenty-seven years and she hadn't enjoyed the experience at all. They were such silly creatures there was no telling what this dentist might do to her.

Looking at the neatly laid out dental instruments did nothing to comfort her. Although she couldn't see any hammers or chisels, several of the implements looked decidedly unpleasant, not at all the kind of things she wanted put into her mouth. Perhaps it had been a mistake allowing the girl to bring her here. If her tooth hadn't been hurting so badly, Fenella knew she would have rushed out there and then.

'Are you sure this is a good idea?' she asked.

'Of course it is. You're not frightened, are you?'

'Vampires are never frightened, Heinz Beans,' Fenella said sternly.

For a moment, the girl couldn't believe her ears. She simply stared at Fenella, her mouth hanging open in amaazement.

'What did you just call me?'

'I called you Heinz Beans.' Fenella felt quite proud of her own cleverness. 'I know it's right because I looked in your bag while you were asleep. Your name was written on all the tins inside.'

'Heinz Beans,' the girl said in wonder, her lips twitching into a smile. 'Heinz Beans!' she repeated, fighting to hold back a giggle.

It was no good. The giggle became a chortle and the chortle became a guffaw. Now it was Fenella's turn to be amazed as she watched the girl roaring with laughter. There was no telling how long she might have continued if she hadn't laughed so much that she gave herself hiccups. While she patted Heinz Beans on the back, Fenella thought once again what strange creatures humans were.

'What was so funny?' Fenella asked once Heinz Beans had recovered. 'Was it something I said?'

'Oh no.' Normally the girl was very honest but she didn't want to hurt Fenella's feelings. Besides, she was trying very hard not to start laughing again. 'I think you're lovely. You're not a bit like I'd have expected a vampire to be.'

There was no chance for them to say anything more because at this moment Mr Pullit came bustling in, a big smile on his face. He was a very friendly man.

'Miss Fang, isn't it?' he asked, seizing hold of Fenella's hand and shaking it vigorously.

Fenella didn't answer. She was too busy looking at her hand, wondering what the dentist had been doing with it. Perhaps pumping her arm up and down helped to loosen her tooth.

'Do sit down,' Mr Pullit went on cheerfully. 'Perhaps you'd like to wait outside, dear.'

'She's staying here with me.' Fenella had grabbed hold of Heinz Beans to stop her leaving. 'I may need her.'

Although Mr Pullit thought this was rather strange, he didn't argue. Normally it was children who wanted grown-ups to stay, not the other way around. He told Heinz Beans to sit on a chair at the side of the room and then turned back to Fenella.

'Right, Miss Fang. Open wide.'

After a moment's hesitation, Fenella stretched her arms out as far as she could. Perhaps the dentist wanted to do some more shaking to make sure the tooth was really loose.

'Very funny, Miss Fang,' Mr Pullit told her. 'I do so like a practical joke but don't let's waste time. Open your mouth as wide as you can.'

When it came to opening their mouths, vampires were rather like snakes – they could open them very wide indeed. Mr Pullit was absolutely delighted. With most people, he was lucky if he could squeeze one hand inside. There was room inside Miss Fang's mouth for both hands and his head as well.

Then Mr Pullit saw what was inside the mouth and he jumped back in alarm, knocking a glass of water from the table beside him. In all his years as a dentist, he had only once seen teeth like Fenella's. The circus had been in town and a vet had asked him to take a look at a lion with a poisoned jaw. And even the lion hadn't had canines and incisors like the ones he was looking at now.

'Jumping jellybeans,' he muttered under his breath. 'What a magnificent set of choppers. Why, she could bite my head off with one snap.'

The dentist was far too fascinated to be nervous for more than a moment. Apart from the size of the teeth, there seemed to be far more of them than there should have been. Leaning closer, Mr Pullit quickly counted them. When he had finished, he was sure he must have made a mistake. He began counting again, ticking them off on his fingers so he wouldn't miss any.

'One, two, three, four, five.'

Mr Pullit didn't get any further because Fenella was becoming fed up. All she wanted was to have the bad tooth removed.

'Save your time,' she said. 'There are forty, just like there should be.'

'No, you've got it wrong, Miss Fang.' Mr Pullit was shaking his head vigorously. 'Thirty-two is the correct number.'

'Stuff and nonsense,' Fenella snapped. 'It's forty.'

The dentist was obviously a fool. All vampires started out with forty teeth. Mr Pullit was about to continue the argument when Heinz Beans decided to take a hand. She could see that Fenella needed her help again.

'Excuse me, Mr Pullit,' she said politely. 'Could I have a word in private with you?'

'Of course you can, my dear.'

He went across to where the girl was sitting and bent down so she could whisper in his ear.

'I'm afraid you have to be very careful with my aunt,' she told him. 'She sometimes has violent turns when she's upset.'

'Does she, indeed?'

The dentist glanced nervously across at Fenella. Like Petunia Pringle, he was wondering whether she ought to be locked up for her own safety – and for the safety of others. Mr Pullit had come across some very strange patients in his time but none of them had been as strange as Miss Fang.

'The thing that upsets her most is remarks about her teeth,' Heinz Beans went on. 'She's very sensitive about them.'

'I'm not surprised. She has far too many of them.'

'I know. It's because her mother was frightened by a shark when she was young.'

Although Mr Pullit thought this was stranger than ever, he decided not to say anything more on the subject. When he went back to Fenella, he was his normal bright and breezy self.

'Right, Miss Fang,' he said jovially. 'Let's have a look at this tooth which is causing all the trouble. Just tell me if this hurts.'

As he spoke, he gently tapped the bad tooth.

'AAAGGGHHH!'

The pain almost made Fenella jump right out of the chair. Her mouth snapped shut so hard that Mr Pullit would have lost his fingers if he hadn't managed to jerk his hand back out of the way.

'Did that hurt?'

'Of course it did, you imbecile. That's why I screamed.'

'Well, at least we know it's the right one.'

'I knew that before.'

Fenella was glaring at the dentist which made him most uncomfortable. She looked as though she was about to become very violent indeed. This made Mr Pullit nervous and he had to use his tie to wipe the sweat from his face.

'I think we'd better have the tooth out right away,' he babbled.

'It's about time,' Fenella growled.

'Will you have an injection or do you prefer gas?'

'She'll have an injection, please.'

Heinz Beans could see that Fenella didn't understand what the dentist was talking about and answered for her. Although she didn't like the look of the needle at all, Fenella didn't make any fuss when she was injected.

'That's fine, Miss Fang,' Mr Pullit said, putting the hypodermic down. 'We'll just wait a few seconds until your gum is numb.'

But Fenella's gum didn't go numb. The end of her nose went numb and her fingers lost their feeling but her gum stayed exactly the same. Not that Fenella minded because she felt marvellous. She was no longer at all nervous and she had quite forgotten about being annoyed with Mr Pullit. In fact, she felt so happy she would have leaned forward and nuzzled his neck if she had been sure her body would move when she wanted it to. Fenella had just discovered that the injection which made human gums go numb didn't work the same way with vampires. It made them completely squiffy instead. Fenella was as drunk as a skunk and she loved it.

'Are you ready to have the tooth removed, Miss Fang?'

For the life of him, the dentist couldn't understand why Miss Fang had such a broad smile all over her face.

'Any time, old bean' Fenella answered. 'I'll just sing you a little song first.'

To Heinz Beans' and Mr Pullit's amazement, Fenella began singing the chorus of 'All you need is teeth', the song which had been top of the vampire hit parade for the last five years. When she had finished, Fenella started clicking loudly, sounding like a bomb which was about to explode. Mr Pullit was sure she must be seriously ill. He didn't know that vampires clicked instead of clapping.

'Are you all right, Miss Fang?' he enquired anxiously.

'I've never felt better, you silly old bat,' Fenella told him, laughing happily. 'I'll do a dance for you if you like.'

'That's very nice of you, I'm sure, but it won't be necessary,' the dentist said quickly. 'I think we'd better see to your tooth.'

'Anything you say, old bean. Pull away, Pullit.'

Fenella thought the joke was so funny, she almost fell out of the chair laughing. Heinz Beans had to come across to help Mr Pullit prop her upright again. By now the dentist was sweating more than ever. He was convinced that he was dealing with a dangerous lunatic and all he wanted was to get rid of her as quickly as possible.

'Open as wide as you can,' he said once Fenella was seated properly.

'Right you are, sport.'

This time Fenella opened so wide her mouth looked like a small cave with teeth. Inside, though, she was already laughing at the new joke she had planned. As Mr Pullit leaned forward, she snapped her teeth together again, narrowly missing his nose. Mr Pullit jumped backwards with a yell of alarm, tripped over his own feet and ended up in an untidy heap on the floor. Fenella thought this was so comical and laughed so much that this time she did fall off the chair, landing on the floor beside Mr Pullit.

'Oh dear, oh dear,' she spluttered. 'You should have seen the expression on your face.'

Unfortunately, Mr Pullit wasn't at all amused. Madwoman or not, he had no intention of allowing this kind of behaviour in his surgery. Heinz Beans was worried too. She couldn't understand what had come over her friend.

'Behave yourself, Fenella,' she whispered as she helped Fenella back into the chair.

'Yes, you behave yourself, Miss Fang,' Mr Pullit said sternly. 'Otherwise I'm afraid you'll have to find yourself another dentist.'

Fenella did her best. Although she would have liked to snap her teeth again, just to see the expression on Mr Pullit's face, she didn't. And although she thought it was very funny being able to look right up the dentist's nose as he bent over her, she managed not to laugh.

I wonder where all those hairs in his nostrils

came from, she thought to herself. They must have grown the wrong way from the top of his head.

By now, Mr Pullit had a firm grip of the bad tooth.

'It will all be over in a minute,' he promised.

But it wasn't. When he tugged at the offending tooth, it didn't move at all. Nor did the dentist have any more success when he tugged harder. It was as though the tooth was set in concrete.

'My, my,' he said, slightly out of breath. 'This is an awkward tooth.'

Fenella simply smiled up at him, her mouth still wide open. She wasn't feeling any pain at all.

Pull it, Pullit, she thought to herself.

She wasn't at all worried that she had made this joke before. It still seemed just as funny. In fact, everything seemed funny to her. Fenella was feeling wonderful.

Mr Pullit was a strong man and he used every bit of his strength as he once more tried to remove the tooth – but it was no good. Although there were one or two creaking sounds from Fenella's jaw, the tooth remained as firmly rooted as ever.

'I'm very sorry, Miss Fang.' This had never happened to Mr Pullit before. 'The tooth doesn't seem to want to come out. I'm not hurting you, am I?'

'Oh no.'

As Fenella's mouth was still open, this sounded rather like a snarl. The dentist was sure she must be angry with him.

'Don't worry, Miss Fang,' he told her. 'We won't be beaten. I'll just have to try harder.'

By now Fenella was so drunk she didn't care what happened to her. This was just as well because Mr Pullit was prepared to do almost anything to remove the tooth. It was the only hope he had of getting the madwoman out of his surgery.

'What I need is more leverage,' he said to himself as he operated the controls on the chair so that Fenella was lying almost flat.

'Excuse me,' Mr Pullit said out loud as he climbed up to kneel on Fenella's stomach. 'Tell me if you're uncomfortable.'

He looked so funny up there that Fenella started laughing again. Poor Mr Pullit was bounced up and down like a small boat in a rough sea.

'Stop it, Miss Fang,' he said, afraid he might be bounced right off. 'You must stay still.'

Fenella did her best but the dentist still wasn't any more successful. Although he pulled and he tugged and he twisted, the tooth remained firmly in Fenella's jaw. Mr Pullit went so red in the face that Fenella became quite worried.

'He'll do himself an injury, straining like that,' she thought. 'I'd better do something to help.'

She reached up with one large hand to take

hold of his arm.

One to be ready, she said to herself, two to get set and three to GO.

On the word GO, Fenella gave a sharp tug and this was all that was needed. The tooth came free so suddenly that Mr Pullit was shot off her stomach like a cork out of a champagne bottle. The dentist went backwards across the surgery like a human rocket, knocking tables and chairs out of the way. He didn't stop until he hit the wall on the far side of the room, banging his head so hard that he saw stars.

'That's done the trick,' Fenella said cheerfully, pushing herself out of the chair and standing unsteadily on her feet. 'Come on, Heinz Beans. Let's go home.'

It wasn't until they had left the surgery that Mr Pullit recovered his senses sufficiently to realize the blood on the roots of the tooth was green, not red. By this time he was past caring anyway. All that mattered was that Miss Fang had gone and he could go back to being a proper dentist again.

Five

It was wonderful not to have toothache any more. For a while Fenella simply lay drowsily in her coffin, thinking back over the events of the previous day. For some reason there were gaps in her memory, parts of the day she couldn't remember, like how she had got back to the crypt, but this didn't matter. She had been to a human dentist; she had pretended to be a human herself without anybody noticing anything strange; and now she didn't have that terrible toothache any longer. Fenella felt very grateful to Heinz Beans for what she had done.

It was some time before she noticed the noise from outside in the crypt. When she listened more carefully, Fenella realized it was the sound of somebody crying.

It must be Heinz Beans, she thought, pushing the lid of the coffin open.

As soon as she sat up, Fenella could see she was right. The girl was curled up in a ball against the wall, sobbing as if her heart would break. Fenella quickly climbed out of the coffin and padded across the crypt.

'What's the matter?' she asked softly.

At least, her voice was soft for a vampire. To a human ear it still sounded pretty terrible and Heinz Beans sat up with a start. When she saw it was Fenella, she tried to brush the tears away with her hands.

'It's nothing,' she mumbled with a sniff.

'Come on, Heinz Beans. You can tell me. I'm your friend.'

Suddenly the girl wasn't crying any more.

'Do you really mean that?'

'Mean what?'

Fenella didn't understand.

'That you're my friend.'

Until Heinz Beans pointed it out to her, Fenella hadn't realized what she had said. The word had just slipped out without thinking. It was quite ridiculous, of course, because no vampire could ever be friends with a human. Or was it so ridiculous? Now she thought about it, Fenella knew she had become fond of the little girl. It was as though their experiences of the previous day had formed a bond between them.

'Yes, Heinz Beans,' Fenella said slowly, amazed at what she was saying. 'I think I do mean it.'

'Oh, Fenella,' the girl cried. 'I'm so happy.'

The girl threw herself into Fenella's arms and gave her a hug. It was the first time Fenella had ever been hugged by a human and, to her surprise, she quite enjoyed it. The child was uncomfortably warm but otherwise it was most pleasant. Fenella almost nuzzled Heinz Bean's neck in return until she remembered that this might frighten the child. After a few seconds, she gently pushed the girl away.

'I want to know why you were crying, Heinz Beans. Perhaps I might be able to help.'

'I wish you could, Fenella.' Now the girl's face was sad again. 'I was thinking about my pet dog, Spot, and how I'm never going to see him again.'

Tears were beginning to well back into the girl's eyes and Fenella could understand how she must feel. She remembered how upset she had been when her own pet bat, Squeak, had died.

'Is he dead?' Fenella asked softly.

'Oh no – he was only a puppy. He was taken away from me and put in the home for unwanted dogs at Deepwell. I do miss him so and I know Spot will be missing me. He's only little and he's never been alone before.

The last few words came out as a wail. Fenella's heart went out to the little girl. She desperately wanted to help her and make her happy again. Fenella thought dogs were nasty, noisy little animals herself but Heinz Beans had obviously loved hers. Suddenly, Fenella realized there might be something she could do after all.

'Did you say Deepwell?' she asked excitedly.

'That's right. It's where the Dogs' Home is.'

'But I know where Deepwell is.' Fenella was becoming more excited by the moment. 'It's only fifty bites from here.'

'Fifty bites?'

Heinz Beans didn't have any idea what Fenella was talking about.

'That's the way us vampires measure distances. Fifty bites would be almost ten of your human mildews.'

'Mildews?' Then the girl realized what Fenella was talking about. 'You mean miles.'

'Something like that,' Fenella said impatiently. 'The thing is, we could go there and get your Spot back.'

'I don't know, Fenella.' The girl wasn't nearly as excited as the vampire. 'I don't think the people at the Dogs' Home would give Spot back to me. I'm not old enough.'

'Who said anything about asking them?' Fenella had it all planned in her mind. 'It's your dog, isn't it?'

'Oh yes. I've had Spot since he was only a few days old. Dad gave him to me.'

'There you are then,' Fenella said triumphantly. 'We'll simply take him back.'

As far as she was concerned, the matter was settled. However, Heinz Beans still wasn't so sure. Ten miles was an awful long way for her little legs.

The fair was only just the other side of Deepwell, yet when she had run away, it had taken all day for her to walk as far as the crypt.

'How will we get there?' she asked doubtfully.

'That's easy,' Fenella answered. 'I'll fly and you can sit on my back. All you'll have to do is hold on tight. Why, we'll have your Spot back in no time at all.'

'Do you really think so?'

Now Heinz Beans was becoming excited too.

'Just leave everything to me,' Fenella said confidently.

It only took a few seconds for Fenella to change into her bat form and arrange the girl comfortably on her back. Vampires were much stronger than humans and Fenella was hardly aware of the extra weight as she soared up into the air.

To begin with, Heinz Beans kept her eyes tightly closed. She hadn't flown before, not even in an aeroplane, and she had never dreamed that one day she might be flying through the night sky on the back of a vampire. However, Fenella flew so steadily that the child soon felt safe enough to look around her. The brightly-lit houses far below seeemed no bigger than matchboxes and she was amazed at how fast the ground was flashing past beneath them. She was sure no aeroplane could travel any faster. It was no time at all before she could see the lights of Deepwell ahead of them.

'Here we are then,' Fenella said over her

shoulder. 'Where exactly is this Dogs' Home of yours?'

'Don't you know where it is?'

'Of course I don't. Vampires don't keep dogs.'

'Well I don't know either. I wasn't allowed to go to the Dogs' Home myself. I just know that's where Spot was taken.'

As they circled over the town, the girl was very close to tears again. She had been so sure it would only be a matter of minutes before she was reunited with her beloved Spot and now her hopes had been dashed. From her seat on Fenella's back, she could see what a large town Deepwell was. There were so many buildings, trying to find the Dogs' Home would be like looking for a needle in a haystack.

'There's only one thing for it, Heinz Beans,' Fenella said. 'I'll land somewhere quiet and you can ask somebody for directions. Can you manage that?'

'Oh yes, Fenella.'

The answer was so obvious that the girl wondered why she hadn't thought of it herself.

Even though it was night time, Bert Bungle was at work. He needed the cover of darkness so nobody could see what he was doing. Bert was a burglar who made his living by breaking into people's houses while they were out and stealing things like

videos, jewellery and any spare cash which might be lying around. At the very moment that Fenella landed, Bert was trying to force open the front window of a house whose owners were on holiday in Majorca. In fact, he was so busy that he didn't hear the footsteps behind him and he didn't realize anybody was there until a hand patted him on the shoulder. Bert was so startled, he jumped three feet straight up into the air, banging his head on the window frame.

'Oh my God,' he yelped. 'It's all a mistake, officer. I was just checking to make sure the window was closed properly. Honest, I was.'

'I'm not an officer,' the girl said.

Bert could see this the moment he turned round. Instead of being pleased to discover that he wasn't under arrest, he became angry instead. Like most burglars, he was a bully as well as a thief.

'What do you think you're doing, sneaking up on me like that?' he demanded fiercely. 'You might have given me a heart attack or palpitations or something.'

'I'm very sorry.' The girl didn't know anything about burglars. She thought Bert must have locked himself out of his own house. 'I only wanted to ask you a question.'

'If I wanted to answer questions, I'd go on Mastermind,' Bert snarled. 'Can't you see I'm busy?'

'It's ever so important.'

'I'll give you important.' Bert raised his hand as though he was about to hit her. 'Just clear off and leave me in peace. And you'd better not tell anybody you've seen me or I'll wring your scrawny little neck.'

Fenella had heard enough. She had been standing in the shadows, keeping out of sight, but now she stepped forward. Nobody was going to bully Heinz Beans like this and get away with it.

At first Bert refused to believe the evidence of his own eyes. It was as though a creature from one of his nightmares had come to life. Policemen were bad enough but this huge bat was something else. He didn't know whether he was more terrified of the glowing eyes or the huge teeth which looked as though they could rip him into shreds. He was so frightened, he almost swallowed his own false teeth.

'Don't you dare talk to my Heinz Beans like that,' Fenella hissed.

Heinz Beans, Bert thought to himself. I must be going mad. I've got bats in the belfry.

'Don't you dare threaten her,' Fenella continued, still moving towards him.

This bat isn't in a belfry, Bert thought. It's right here and it's going to do something horrible to me unless I clear off fast.

The burglar turned to run but Fenella moved much faster. He only managed one step before a claw descended on his shoulder, pinching painfully into the flesh. Although Bert was a large man, Fenella lifted him from the ground as though he were a toy. She held him high in the air while she shook him, making his teeth rattle like castanets.

'Tell Heinz Beans you're sorry,' she ordered.

'I-I-I'm-m-m s-s-sorr-sorry, H-H-Heinz B-B-Beans.' He was being shaken so hard that the words wobbled in Bert's mouth.

'That's much better.' Although Fenella didn't put Bert down, she did stop shaking him. 'Now tell Heinz Beans that you'll be happy to answer her question for her.'

'I'll be happy to answer your question for you, Heinz Beans,' Bert gabbled.

He would have promised anything if this meant the monstrous bat wouldn't hurt him.

'Thank you,' the girl said. 'That's very nice of you. All I want to know is where the Dogs' Home is.'

Luckily, Bert did know. He had burgled a house in the next road only the week before and he rattled off the directions as fast as he could.

'Can I go now, please?' he asked fearfully once he had finished.

'In a moment.' Fenella was still holding him high above the ground. 'Just remember one thing. Don't tell anybody what you've seen tonight.'

'I won't. I promise.'

'Make sure you remember.' Fenella snapped her teeth together close to Bert's face. He was trembling so much, his whole body quivered like a badly set blancmange. 'If you do tell anybody, I shall be back to see you some other night.'

This was the very last thing Bert wanted. When Fenella dropped him, his legs were already running before they touched the ground. And as he ran Bert was promising himself that he would find some other kind of work. He knew he would never dare go out after dark again.

Fenella and the girl could hear where the Dogs' Home was long before they actually saw it. However, the frenzied barking suddenly died away as Fenella swooped over. Dogs didn't like vampires. In fact, they were even more frightened by them than humans like Bert were. As Fenella's shadow passed over them, all the dogs fell silent, apart from one old Airedale who was blind and didn't know she was there. The others crawled on their bellies into the corners of their pens, whining softly to themselves as they tried to hide.

Neither Fenella nor the girl had realized quite how big the Dogs' Home would be. From the air they could see that there were hundreds of pens, filled with every possible kind of dog. There were Afghans and affenpinschers, bassets and beagles, Chihuahuas and collies, dachshunds and Dobermans, not to mention every sort of mongrel imaginable. There was even one Erz Mountains Dachsbracke which had smuggled itself aboard a coach in Austria and got lost in Deepwell. Heinz Beans could feel her heart sinking as she looked at the thousands of dogs below her.

'We'll never find Spot among all those,' she said despairingly.

'Stuff and nonsense. Absolute balderdash.' Fenella wasn't about to give up now. 'We can look together. It won't take us long, you'll see. What does this Spot look like?'

'Oh, you can't miss him, Fenella. Spot is the loveliest, most cuddly little puppy you ever saw. He's a Dalmatian, white with black spots, and his tail is always wagging.'

'Right you are, Heinz Beans,' Fenella said, looking around for a place to land. 'We'll have him back with you in no time.'

But they didn't. Fenella took the right hand side of the kennel area while the girl searched the left. Between them they looked in every single pen and there was no sign of Spot. After an hour, there was nowhere left to look and even Fenella was becoming despondent.

'Are you sure Spot was brought here?' she asked.

'I know he was. Cousin Fred told me. He said he would have to stay here for the rest of his life unless he found a new owner.'

There was a note of desperation in her voice. Fenella turned to take another look around her but it was no good. There were no more pens for them to search.

'Oh Spot,' the girl wailed. 'Where are you?'

As if in answer to the question, they both heard an excited yapping. Although it was muffled, they could hear it clearly.

'It's Spot. I'm sure it is.' The girl was jumping up and down with delight. 'Good boy, Spot. Bark again. It's me. I've come to fetch you.'

The puppy barked again and there was a scratching noise, as though he was trying to get out of a door. The sound came from a small hut which stood apart from the pens and Heinz Beans' feet almost flew across the ground as she rushed towards it. When she tried the door handle, though, there was another disappointment.

'It's locked,' she cried. 'I can't get in.'

On the other side of the door, the barking became more excited than ever. Spot's claws were scrabbling at the wood as though he could force his way through.

'Leave it to me,' Fenella said.

When she pulled at the handle, there was a crunching sound as the lock shattered and the hut door began to swing open. An overjoyed white and black bundle came hurtling out through the widening crack, leaping straight into the girl's arms. His tail was wagging so hard that his entire body shook and he licked Heinz Beans so vigorously that she was in danger of losing her skin. Heinz Beans was shedding tears of delight and the sight of the two of them together brought a lump to Fenella's throat.

'Come on,' she said gruffly. 'We'd better get going before somebody finds us.'

Six

Now that Fenella and Heinz Beans were friends there was no need for Fenella to leave the crypt, and over the next few nights the two of them settled into a routine. The girl took to sleeping during the daytime so she could be awake at the same time as Fenella, and at night they travelled anywhere they wanted. With Heinz Beans and Spot sitting on her back, Fenella flew all over the place. One night they sat on the roof of Buckingham Palace to watch the changing of the guard. On another they had a picnic at the very top of the Eiffel Tower while Paris slept below them. After Heinz Beans had mentioned something about Concorde, Fenella decided to show off her own speed. She took the little girl all the way to New York to see the skyscrapers, getting back to the crypt shortly before first light.

In short, the two of them had a wonderful time together. For Heinz Beans it was like having a mother, sister and friend all rolled into one, even if the one was a vampire. As for Fenella, she soon found it difficult to remember what it had been like living in the crypt all on her own. It was such a pleasure to have Heinz Beans's smiling face awaiting her every night when she climbed out of her coffin.

Even Spot enjoyed himself. He was back with his mistress and he had one of Fenella's old shrouds to curl up on when he was tired. He soon became almost as fond of Fenella as Heinz Beans was. Spot only ever licked Fenella once because she tasted rather horrid, but he made up for this by wagging his tail a lot whenever he saw her.

However, like all good things, it had to finish some time. The beginning of the end came the same night as their visit to New York. Fenella was tired after the long flight and she was about to climb into her coffin when she suddenly remembered something.

'Heinz Beans,' she said. 'I haven't seen you eat anything tonight.'

'I know. I wasn't feeling hungry.'

'You must have something,' Fenella told her. 'Otherwise you'll make yourself ill.'

'Perhaps I'll have a bite to eat once you're in your coffin.'

Tired as she was, Fenella knew something was wrong. Heinz Beans was normally such an honest child yet now she was avoiding her friend's eye, as though she had something to hide. For a moment Fenella was puzzled. Then the answer occurred to her and she walked quickly across the crypt to where Heinz Beans's bag was leaning against the wall. When she looked inside, she could see there was only one tin left.

'Is this all the food you have?' she demanded, holding up the tin.

Fenella was angry with herself. It was something she should have thought of before.

'Yes, Fenella,' the girl's voice was very small. 'I was saving it for Spot. I'm not at all hungry myself, honestly.'

'Stuff and nonsense.' Fenella might not know a great deal about human children but she did know they needed plenty of food. 'You're going to eat some of these now and I'm not getting into my coffin until you have. Tomorrow night we'll go and get you some more.'

'But I haven't got any money.'

The girl had been worrying about her dwindling store of food for days and her voice was almost a wail. After she had explained about money and shops to her friend, Fenella could see the problem for herself. It was a very troubled vampire who eventually climbed into her coffin. And Fenella would have been even more concerned if she had known what had been happening at Blood Castle.

As he had grown older, Samuel Suck's memory had grown worse and worse. At times it was downright terrible. One night he had forgotten how to open his coffin lid and he had had to stay inside until Igor came to release him. On another night he had nearly jumped off the castle battlements without changing into his bat form. And when he did change, he discovered that he had forgotten how to fly. Samuel might have hurt himself quite badly if Igor hadn't been standing beneath the battlements at the time.

The most irritating thing about Samuel's failing memory was that on occasions he knew he had forgotten something important and simply couldn't remember what it was. Sometimes it would be nights and nights before it finally came back to him.

It had been like this for the past night or two. Samuel knew there was something important he should have done but he simply couldn't remember what. Although he spent hours racking his brains, it was no good. All he knew was that what he had forgotten had something to do with the spare coffin. The best he could do was ring his bell to summon his servant.

'Why am I thinking about the spare coffin, Igor?' he asked.

'I don't know, Master.' Igor had become used to strange questions like this. 'Perhaps your old one is draughty again. I'll go down and see if there are any holes in it.'

'No, no, no,' Samuel said impatiently. He

should have known that talking to Igor was about as useful as talking to a brick wall. 'I had the feeling I'd invited somebody to stay.'

'Not that I know of, Master, unless you changed your mind about having another party.'

After the mess the guests had made last Hallowe'en, Samuel had vowed never to have another.

'No, it wasn't that.'

'In that case, I can't help you, Master. It's a shame Miss Fenella never came back. I'm sure she could soon have put you straight.'

As soon as Igor mentioned Fenella's name, Samuel remembered everything. Fenella had been in trouble, something to do with a human, and she had intended to stay at Blood Castle until she found a new home. Samuel cursed his memory under his breath. As she hadn't returned, his niece could be in serious trouble.

'Fenella did say she was coming to stay, didn't she?'

'That's right, Master. That's why I made the spare coffin ready for her.'

'But she didn't come back. Has there been any message?'

'Not that I know of, Master.'

'Well, why didn't you remind me before.'

'I didn't know you'd forgotten, Master. You didn't say anything about reminding you.'

Old Samuel sighed in exasperation. Although

he was very fond of Igor, there were times when he was sure his servant was an absolute idiot. Igor seemed to have solid bone between his large ears instead of brains.

'There could be something wrong with Fenella.' Now there was a quaver in the old vampire's voice. Fenella was his favourite niece and he couldn't bear to think of anything happening to her. 'You'd better get over to her crypt and make sure she's all right.'

'Right you are, Master.' Igor touched where his forelock would have been if he had had any hair. 'I'll set out first thing in the morning.'

Even though this was the best he could do, Samuel tossed and turned in his coffin for most of the next day. He was far too worried about Fenella to be able to sleep. When he did eventually climb wearily out of his coffin that night, he found he was at a loose end. There was no Igor for him to talk to and he was too concerned about his niece to do any inventing.

'I know,' he muttered to himself. 'I'll teach myself to fly again.'

This was something he had been meaning to do for some time. Being the only vampire in the world who didn't have any teeth was bad enough without being unable to fly as well.

For an hour or two Samuel practised jumping off the table and cupboards in the Great Hall.

Although he thought he was doing quite well, it was very difficult for him to tell. He was so close to the ground when he jumped that Samuel wasn't sure whether he was really flying or not.

'I need somewhere higher,' he said. 'Not too high, though, in case I can't fly and I hurt myself.'

The perfect place to try was directly above him. For a few seconds Samuel gazed up at the huge

oak beams near the ceiling of the Great Hall. Then, smiling happily to himself, he went off to find a ladder.

It took Igor a whole day and most of a night to cover the distance Fenella had flown in a few minutes. This wasn't simply because it was a long way. With his different-sized legs, Igor couldn't walk very fast and it took him twice as long as it would have taken anybody else. It was all right in towns and villages where he could walk with one foot on the pavement and the other in the road but where there was no pavement it was very difficult for Igor to keep in a straight line. He was always stumbling into barbed wire fences or falling into ditches and this did nothing to improve his already foul temper. Igor was bad-tempered even when he was feeling happy.

Just before dawn, Igor eventually arrived in the graveyard. He had no sooner settled himself in a small copse of trees near the crypt than he spotted a fast-moving shape approaching him through the dark sky. He recognized what it was immediately.

'It's Miss Fenella,' Igor said happily, dribbling with pleasure. 'She's safe after all.'

Igor started to rise to his feet to wave a greeting. Then he noticed that Fenella wasn't alone and he dropped down into hiding again. There were a girl and a dog riding on the vampire's back! As far as the dismayed Igor was concerned, this could only mean one thing.

'Oh no.' Igor shook his head in disbelief, spraying the grass and leaves around him with dandruff. 'Poor Miss Fenella has been taken prisoner. That horrible little girl has managed to capture her. I'd better get back and tell Master Suck at once.'

On his return journey, Igor was a quarter of a mile down the road when he fell into a ditch. It was a particularly deep ditch, full of particularly dirty water, and some of the words Igor used weren't at all pleasant. However, it was while he was standing beside the ditch, dripping wet and with duckweed draped around his ears, that the thought occurred to him.

'It's going to take a day and a night to get back to Blood Castle,' he muttered. 'And Master Suck can't fly no more so that means another day and a night to come back here again. That makes—'

While he tried to work out the tricky sum, Igor's brow creased into a frown, making his hideous face even more hideous than usual. Frowning didn't seem to help so Igor tried scratching his head instead. All that happened then was that he got dandruff and duckweed in his eyes.

'That makes a lot of days and nights,' Igor finished, giving up the tricky sum. 'It's far too long. Anything could have happened to Miss Fenella by then.'

Igor's brain worked very slowly and he continued to walk while he considered the problem. Half a mile further on he lurched into a barbed wire fence, pricking himself most painfully. This time Igor's language was even worse but the answer to the problem came to him while he was still unhooking himself.

'I ought to sort things out myself,' he said. 'I could deal with that whippersnapper easily.'

The more he thought about it, the more Igor liked the idea. He hardly felt it when he pricked a thumb on one of the barbs.

'Miss Fenella and Master Suck should have listened to me in the first place,' he went on. 'There's only one thing to do with the interfering busybody and I'm the man to do it.'

There was a horrible leer on Igor's face as he headed back towards the graveyard. He would have a well-earned rest and then he would rescue Fenella. Igor was already looking forward to it.

'Go away, Spot,' Fenella mumbled sleepily.

It was only just dark and she was still tired after the long journey to New York. But Spot wouldn't go away. He continued to bark frantically and scratch at the side of the coffin.

Suddenly Fenella was wide awake. She had heard Spot when he was playing or pretending to be fierce but she had never before heard him bark quite like this. Besides, Heinz Beans would never allow the puppy to make this much noise while her friend was sleeping. Fenella knew there must be something dreadfully wrong and she threw open the lid of the coffin with a crash.

'Heinz Beans,' she called. 'Where are you?'

There was no answer and when Fenella looked around, she couldn't see the child anywhere in the crypt. There was only Spot, who was still jumping up and down and barking frantically. It was almost as though the puppy was trying to tell her something.

'Good boy, Spot,' Fenella said, clambering quickly out of the coffin. 'Where's Heinz Beans?'

The puppy immediately started towards the exit from the crypt, looking back over his shoulder to make sure Fenella was following. The puppy seemed to be limping slightly but Fenella was too worried about her friend to wonder why. It was dark outside in the graveyard and Spot stopped, sniffing the air to try to locate his mistress. Even with her vampire eyes, Fenella could see no sign of the girl.

'Heinz Beans,' she called desperately. 'What's happened to you?'

Her only answer was a terrified scream which further chilled Fenella's cold blood. It came from a nearby copse of trees and as soon as she looked in this direction Fenella could distinguish two figures struggling in the shadows. The smaller of the two figures was Heinz Beans. She was fighting to free herself from the cruel grip of a man, a large, misshapen man whom Fenella recognized at once.

'Igor,' she hissed.

When a vampire wants to move fast, it can move very fast indeed. Fenella was no more than a blur as she raced towards the trees, leaving Spot far behind. Even so, she had only covered half the distance when Heinz Beans screamed again, making the hairs on the nape of Fenella's neck stand on end. The girl was clearly scared out of her wits.

'Be quiet, you snivelling brat,' Igor growled, raising his hand to hit her.

But the blow didn't land. Igor had been too busy to see Fenella coming and for a few seconds he had no idea what was happening to him. One moment he was about to hit the girl. The next he was being lifted high into the air by his large ear.

'My ear,' he shrieked. 'You're pulling off my—'

The sentence was never finished because it was Igor's turn to scream as Fenella started to swing him around her head.

'Let go,' he managed to bellow. 'Let go of my ear.'

And Fenella did let go. For a few seconds, as he sailed through the still night air, Igor knew what it was like to fly, but his brief flight came to an abrupt end when he crashed into one of the gravestones. He hit it so hard that his head made a large, dandruff-flecked dent in the stone.

'Are you all right, Heinz Beans?' Fenella asked anxiously.

'I think so.'

Although she was still trembling from her fright, the girl knew she was safe now that Fenella was there.

'Thank goodness for that. Just wait here for a moment. I'll be right back.'

Igor was still struggling to his feet, clutching the bump on his head, when Fenella arrived in front of him. She was so angry that sparks appeared to be flashing from her eyes.

'What do you think you were doing?' she hissed.

Her voice was so terrible that Igor cringed away from her. He had never seen Fenella so furious before.

'I was only trying to help, Miss Fenella. I was going to kill the girl and—'

'You were going to do what?'

'Kill the girl, Miss Fenella, and—'

For the second time in as many minutes, Igor was flying – only this time he travelled much further and landed much harder. He had to check with both hands to make sure his ear was still attached to his head. And Fenella hadn't finished

with Igor yet. She was towering over him again
while he was on his knees.

'Please, Mistress,' Igor sobbed. 'Don't pick me
up by my ear again.'

Fenella used his nose instead, holding him so
that his feet dangled well above the ground. Her
face was so close to his that all Igor could see
was teeth.

'Listen to me, you miserable microbe,' she
hissed. 'That little girl is my friend.'

'Yeth, Mithtreth.'

It was very difficult for Igor to speak while he
was being held by his nose.

'If you ever lay a finger on her again,' Fenella
continued, 'it will be the last thing you do. Is that
clearly understood?'

'Yeth, Mithtreth. I underthtand, Mithtreth.'

'You'd better.' Still holding him by the nose,
Fenella shook Igor so hard that his brain rattled
around inside his skull like a pea in a saucepan. 'I
shan't warn you again.'

Fenella dropped him to the ground and Igor
immediately scuttled away on his hands and
knees to cower behind the nearest gravestone.
With one final glare in his direction, Fenella
turned on her heel. However, she had only taken
two steps when Igor spoke.

'Pleathe, Mithtreth.' Although Fenella was no
longer holding it, Igor's nose was so swollen that
he still couldn't speak properly. 'May I thay

thomething, Mithtreth?'

'What is it, Igor?' Fenella asked impatiently.

She wanted to check that Heinz Beans was all right.

'Do you promithe not to hurt me again, Mithtreth?'

'I promise.'

'Well, Mithtreth, your little friend ith a—'

For some reason Igor stopped.

'Get on with it, for goodness sake.' Fenella was more impatient than ever. 'Just spit it out.'

'ThegirlithadangerouthcriminalMithtreth.'

Igor gabbled the words out so fast that they all joined together into one. As soon as he had finished, he ducked down behind the gravestone.

'What was that? It sounded as if you said the girl was a dangerous criminal.'

'Thatth right, Mith Fenella.' Igor was cautiously peering over the top of the gravestone. 'There were polithe pothters up in all the townth and villageth. They had her photograph on.'

'Are you sure?'

Whatever else he might be, Fenella knew Igor wasn't a liar.

'Yeth, Mithtreth. I recognithed her the moment I went into the crypt.'

'What did these posters say?'

'They thaid . . .' Igor screwed his ugly face into a hideous frown while he tried to remember, '. . . thatth right, they thaid HAVE YOU THEEN THITH.'

97

'Is that all?'

The message didn't seem to make sense.

'Oh no, Mith Fenella, there wath more but I wath in a hurry. Bethideth, all that reading wath making my head hurt.'

Reading wasn't one of the things which Igor did best. It had taken him twenty-five minutes to spell out HAVE YOU SEEN THIS.

For a few seconds Fenella was baffled. She knew that Igor must have seen the posters but she was equally certain that Heinz Beans wasn't a criminal. Then she realized what the posters must be for and her face became grim.

'Wait here until I call you, Igor,' she said. 'I may need you later.'

She was already walking away before she had finished speaking, heading back to where Spot was contentedly licking the little girl's face.

Seven

'Listen, Heinz Beans,' Fenella said later that night. 'I hate having to say this, but you can't stay here any longer.'

'Why?' The girl looked as though she had been hit. 'Don't you like me any more?'

'No, child, it isn't anything like that. I enjoy having you here but a crypt is meant for vampires, not humans. For a start, you and Spot don't have any food left. What are you going to eat?'

There was no answer to this and the girl kept quiet.

'Besides,' Fenella went on, 'it's nearly the end of your summer. Very soon the nights will be too cold for you.'

'I'll wear all my clothes at once,' Heinz Beans told her. 'I can do exercises to keep warm.'

'That's silly and you know it. In any case, there's your father to think of. How do you think he must feel if he's heard you're missing? And what about your aunt and uncle? I know for a fact that they are very worried.'

'You do?'

The girl's voice was very small.

'I'm afraid so. They must have been to the police to report your disappearance. Igor tells me there are posters up all over the area with your photograph on, asking if anybody has seen you.'

'Oh dear.'

Heinz Beans's voice was smaller than ever. She had only just realized how selfish she had been. When she had decided to run away, she hadn't stopped to think about the effects on other people.

'I think we have some talking to do,' Fenella continued. She hated to see Heinz Beans so miserable but she knew what she was doing was right. 'Now might be a very good time to explain exactly why you did run away.'

'Do I have to?'

'Yes, Heinz Beans, you do.' Fenella sounded very firm. 'I can't help you unless I know exactly what happened.'

Although Heinz Beans began slowly and uncertainly, once she had started the whole story soon came pouring out. After keeping it bottled up inside her for so long, it was a relief to have everything in the open. Some of it Fenella knew already, and some of it she had guessed, but most of what the girl had to say was completely new to her.

The trouble had begun when Heinz Beans's father was given a job in Nigeria. As it had been impossible to take his daughter with him, he had had to leave her with her aunt and uncle for the six months he would be away.

'What about your mother?' Fenella interrupted.

'I haven't got one,' Heinz Beans told her. 'She was killed in a car accident while I was still a baby.'

Although Heinz Beans had known she would miss her father, she hadn't been at all worried about staying with her Aunt May and Uncle Albert. She was very fond of both of them and she had thought it might be fun living in the fair they owned. And so it had been at first, especially as her aunt and uncle had treated her as though she was their own child. In fact, the only fly in the ointment had been Cousin Fred. He was several years older than Heinz Beans and until she went to stay at the fair she had had no idea what a mean and unpleasant boy he could be.

'What did he do?' Fenella asked. 'Did he bully you?'

'Not really,' Heinz Beans answered. 'He never hit me or anything like that. Fred was just mean and horrible. He was always telling me that Dad would never come back from Nigeria. He said he'd be eaten by cannibals or trampled by an elephant or something. He seemed to think it was funny when he made me cry.'

'Why didn't you tell his mother or father what he was doing?'

'Dad always told me I ought to stick up for myself, not tell tales. Besides, Aunt May and Uncle Albert probably wouldn't have believed me. Fred was always as nice as pie when they were around. He was only nasty to me when we were on our own.'

'I see.'

'But you don't, Fenella.' Heinz Beans was fighting hard to keep the tears from her eyes. 'I could put up with what Fred did to me, even if it wasn't very nice. It was what he did to poor Spot that I couldn't bear. He hated dogs and he took it out on Spot. Once Fred tied a firework to his tail while he was asleep and then lit it. Spot was so terrified that he shook for hours. Another time Fred put pepper all over his bone. Spot sneezed so much his eyes nearly popped out.'

'How beastly.'

Fenella had grown very fond of Spot.

'The trouble was, Fred made Aunt May and Uncle Albert think Spot was a naughty dog. Fred was always tearing things up or breaking them and then saying Spot had done it. In the end, Aunt May said Spot had to be kept tied up. Spot absolutely hated it. He used to howl all night.'

'Was that why he was sent to the Dogs' Home?'

'No, that was because he bit Fred. Fred kept tormenting and hurting him and Spot gave him a little nip because he was so frightened. Of course, Fred told his parents that Spot had attacked him for no reason at all. That was when they said Spot had to go. They said it wasn't safe to keep him in case he attacked somebody else. When Spot went, I decided to go too. I didn't stop to think how much worry I'd be causing. All I wanted was to get a long way away from Fred.'

After Heinz Beans had finished, Fenella was silent for a while. She thought Cousin Fred sounded as unpleasant as some of the humans in the story-books she had read when she was young.

'You do like your aunt and uncle, don't you?' she said at last.

'Oh yes, they're lovely,' Heinz Beans told her.

'So that just leaves Cousin Fred. Perhaps we can think of something to make him see the error of his ways.' There was a smile on Fenella's lips which would have had Fred quaking in his shoes if he had been there to see it. 'I think it's high time you met my Uncle Samuel, Heinz Beans. He'll know what to do if anyone does. Come on. Let's go and collect Igor and we'll all fly up to Blood Castle together.'

Fenella had already started towards the door when Heinz Beans stopped her by catching hold of her arm.

'I know I have to go back, Fenella.' Two large tears were trickling down the girl's cheeks. 'It's the only thing I can do to stop everybody worrying about me. But there's something you've forgotten. When I do go back, I won't see you any more. I'll miss you terribly.'

'Stuff and nonsense, child. I'll come and visit you every night if that's what you want, but we can arrange that later. There's Cousin Fred to sort out first.'

For some reason, Fenella seemed to have a lump in her own throat. She knew she would miss Heinz Beans as well.

With Igor on her back as well as Heinz Beans and the puppy, Fenella had a full load aboard and it was a relief to land on the battlements of Blood Castle. At first both Heinz Beans and Spot had been nervous about being so close to Igor. However, after Igor had apologized and Fenella had explained that he didn't really mean any harm, they felt much better. Even the smell wasn't too bad if they kept their noses pointing away from him.

'Come on, everybody,' Fenella said. 'Let's find Uncle Samuel. He should be up and about by now.'

On her own, Heinz Beans would have found the gloomy old castle very frightening. With Fenella beside her she felt perfectly safe, and, as they wound their way down the spiral staircase, she was quite excited at the thought of meeting the oldest vampire in the world. Unfortunately, he was nowhere to be found. Although they went through all the rooms calling out his name, there was absolutely no sign of Uncle Samuel.

'Oh dear,' Fenella said anxiously. 'I do hope nothing has happened to him'

'There's no need to worry, Miss Fenella,' Igor told her. 'I should have thought of it before. The Master has forgotten how to open his coffin again. You wait here, Miss, and I'll pop down to the dungeon to let him out.'

The servant was only gone for a couple of minutes and when he returned his hideous face was creased into a worried frown.

'He's not there, Mistress. The coffin lid is open but there's no Master. I can't think what can have happened to him.'

Nor could Fenella. She knew Uncle Samuel wouldn't have left the castle – he hadn't been out visiting ever since he had forgotten how to fly. She was certain something dreadful must have happened to him.

'What's that funny noise?' Heinz Beans asked suddenly.

Now the girl had mentioned it, Fenella could hear the strange bubbling sound too.

'I don't know,' she answered. 'Igor, is your tummy rumbling again?'

'No, Miss Fenella. It must be the drains.'

'It isn't,' Heinz Beans said excitedly, pointing up towards the ceiling. 'Is that your Uncle Samuel up there?'

They all looked upwards. Sure enough, Samuel Suck was lying on one of the beams near the hall ceiling. He was fast asleep and the bubbling noise was the sound of his snores.

'Silly old thing,' Fenella said fondly, feeling most relieved. 'I wonder what he's doing there?'

'I'll wake him up and ask him, Mistress.'

Igor had already picked up a heavy jug from the table beside him. He was about to throw it at Samuel when Fenella grabbed hold of his arm.

'Don't do that. You might knock him off.'

'I'm sorry, Miss Fenella. I didn't think of that.'

He put the jug down again.

'It's no good shouting,' Fenella said, peering upwards. 'He'll never hear us. I suppose I'd better fly up and wake him myself.'

'Wait a minute, Mistress,' Igor had just noticed the long ladder on the floor. 'I can use that. I'll have the Master down in to time at all.'

'Well do be careful,' Fenella warned him as he scuttled forward to pick up the ladder.

'Don't you worry your pretty little head about it, Miss Fenella. The Master will be down in a jiffy.'

Everything would have been all right if it hadn't

been for Igor's legs. Although it was a very heavy ladder, the servant could lift it easily enough. The trouble started when he tried to walk with it. As soon as he stepped on to his short leg, the ladder began to sway dangerously.

'Look out,' Fenella and Heinz Beans shouted together, watching the top of the ladder swing towards the beam where Samuel was sleeping.

'It's all right.' Igor had stepped up on to his long leg and the ladder swung away again. 'I can manage,' he went on, dropping down on to his shorter leg.

This time the top of the ladder swung much further, so far that it caught Samuel in the ribs and knocked him from the beam. They all watched in horror as the old vampire tumbled through the air towards the hard flagstones, still snoring as he fell. Although Fenella had started foward, she knew she would never be in time to break his fall.

Heinz Beans couldn't bear to watch. She was about to close her eyes so she wouldn't see him crash to the floor when a marvellous thing happened. Samuel's body began to change as he plummeted downwards. His hands and feet became claws and great wings sprouted where his arms had been. Just when it seemed certain that nothing could save him, old Samuel suddenly soared upwards again, flapping his wings powerfully.

'I did it,' he cackled in triumph. 'Dracula's teeth, I really did it.'

For the next few seconds, the delighted Samuel flew all round the hall. One moment he would swoop low over their heads, making them duck, and the next he soared back to the ceiling. After he had eventually landed and changed from his bat form, his old face was crinkled into a broad smile.

'Did you all see me?' he chortled. 'I can fly again. I knew I could do it. Why, it's as easy as . . . as easy as. . . .'

'As easy as falling off a beam, Uncle?' Fenella suggested.

Samuel didn't mind at all when Fenella, Heinz Beans and Igor burst out laughing at him. He was so happy that he joined in the laughter himself.

Everybody had a lot of explaining to do. Samuel Suck had to tell the others how he had accidentally knocked the ladder down and had waited on the beam until somebody arrived to rescue him. It had seemed awfully high there and he still hadn't been sure he could really fly. After he had finished, Igor had to explain to Samuel how he had knocked him off the beam, and Fenella told him why she hadn't returned to Blood Castle to use the spare coffin. Last of all, it was left to Heinz Beans to explain why she had run away and moved into Fenella's crypt.

'Well, Heinz Beans,' Samuel said thoughtfully after he had heard the whole story. 'It's not often we have a human visitor at Blood Castle. Normally you wouldn't be very welcome here but if you're a friend of Fenella's, that makes you a friend of mine.'

'Thank you, sir,' Heinz Beans said politely.

'It seems to me that you have quite a problem, young lady. Did you have any thoughts about what we could do, Fenella?'

'Not really, Uncle. I suppose I could frighten this Cousin Fred so much that he wouldn't dare be nasty to Heinz Beans again.'

'That's a good idea, Miss Fenella,' Igor broke in excitedly, beginning to dribble. 'There's no need for you to bother, though. I could do it for you. I'd take my knife with me and I'd prick him a little and . . . and . . . and I'm very sorry, Master.'

Igor had just noticed the way Samuel was glaring at him. He knew this meant it was high time for him to shut up.

'I should think so too, Igor,' Samuel said sternly. 'Frightening the boy is no real answer on its own. I'm sure it would work but then he would be nice to young Heinz Beans here for all the wrong reasons.'

'That's what I thought too,' Fenella told him. 'I was sure you'd be able to come up with something better.'

'I'll do my best, my dear,' Old Samuel was smiling delightedly again. There was nothing he enjoyed more than a compliment. 'Here's what I suggest you do.'

All the others leaned forward to listen as Samuel started to explain his plan. When he finally stopped, everybody was smiling. Even Spot was wagging his tail.

It was a cold, rainy night and all the customers seemed to have gone home. Most of the stalls had closed already and Fred decided he might as well shut down the coconut shy too. He was about to pick up the first of the wooden shutters when he noticed a man approaching. Although the stranger was in the shadows, Fred knew at once that there was something odd about him. Instead of walking in a straight line, the man was lurching all over the place.

He must be drunk, Fred thought, as he watched the man bump off the wall of the fortune teller's stall and splash through the middle of a large puddle.

When the man came forward into the light, Fred caught a glimpse of his face and the sight sent a shiver down his spine. He had never seen anybody quite so ugly in his life. Just looking at him made Fred feel ill.

'Is something the matter, boy?'

The man had stopped at the stall. Close up, he was even more hideous and he smelled as though he had been rolling in manure.

'Oh no, sir,' Fred stammered.

'Then why are you staring? Bowled over by my good looks, are you?'

'Yes, sir. I'm sorry, sir.'

Igor laughed unpleasantly and picked up one of the wooden balls. He had never been to a fair before so he wasn't sure what it was for.

'What do you do with this?' he demanded.

'You throw the balls at the coconut, sir.' Without really knowing why, Fred was beginning to be frightened. 'If you knock one off, you win a prize.'

Although he didn't say so, Igor thought this sounded rather boring. You couldn't hurt a coconut and the prizes – goldfishes, fluffy teddy bears – didn't look very interesting. Igor would have far preferred a Do-It-Yourself torture kit. All the same, he threw the ball at one of the coconuts. He hit it but the coconut didn't fall from its stand.

'It's a swindle.' Igor was outraged. 'Those coconuts are stuck down.'

'No, they're not, sir. Look.' Fred went to lift the coconut up from the stand. 'You have to hit the hairy bit at the top.'

'And then I'll get a prize?'

'You're almost sure to— OUCH!'

Igor had thrown another ball. This one had bounced off Fred's head.

'Do I win a prize now?' Igor asked with an evil smile.

'Of course you don't.' Fred was more frightened than ever and very close to tears. 'You hit my head, not the coconut.'

'Well, your head is hairy and it looks like a coconut to me.'

Igor was very pleased with his little joke and he was laughing out loud as he threw yet another ball. If Fred hadn't ducked, this one would have hit him on the head too.

'Please stop it, sir.' Fred was crying by now. 'You're supposed to throw the balls at the coconuts.'

'It's much more fun throwing them at you,' Igor said with a horrible leer. 'Nasty, mean children like you deserve to be hurt.'

This was when Fred decided he wanted to be somewhere else, somewhere where there were people who could protect him from this madman. Igor had snatched up another handful of balls but Fred didn't wait for him to throw them. Instead, he pushed open the door at the back of the stall and ran out into the deserted, rain-splashed fairground. Behind him, Fred could hear the sounds of Igor scrambling over the counter after him.

Fred ran for his life, not caring about the puddles he splashed through. He had hoped there might be somebody to help him but all the other stalls were deserted, standing dark and empty in the rain. He seemed to be completely alone in the fairground apart from the man running along behind him. When he glanced back over his shoulder, Fred was amazed at how fast Igor was moving. Although he couldn't travel in a straight line, he was scuttling along much faster than the terrified boy in front. Fred knew he would be caught long before he reached safety and the knowledge made him sob with fear.

'Help,' he cried desperately. 'Help me some-body. I'm being – OUCH – chased by a dangerous – OUCH – maniac.'

Igor was throwing balls as he ran and his aim was remarkably good.

'Help,' Fred tried again. 'Please – OUCH – help me.'

Although he didn't dare look back over his shoulder again, Fred knew the man was only a few paces behind him. He was as good as caught.

'Quickly, Fred. Over here.'

The girl's voice had come from his right and, when Fred looked, he could see that the lights had come on in front of the Ghost Train. A small figure was standing on the steps, waving him towards her. Fred was far too scared to wonder where his cousin had appeared from. All he knew was that there was somebody prepared to help him.

He ran towards her as he had never run before.

His feet almost seemed to fly over the rain-soaked ground but he could still hear the uneven slip-slop-slap of Igor's feet close behind him.

'Quickly, Fred,' Heinz Beans shouted again. 'Jump into one of the cars. You'll be safe inside.'

Without thinking Fred bounded up the steps and scrambled into the front car of the Ghost Train. No sooner had his bottom touched the seat than Heinz Beans pressed a switch and the train started. Although Igor was close enough to jump into one of the cars himself, he didn't. He stopped beside the girl and watched the Ghost Train vanish from sight.

'Did I do all right?' he asked, wiping his dripping nose on the back of his hand.

'You were magnificent,' Heinz Beans told him. 'Thank you.'

'Well, I'd better be off now. I don't like to leave Master Suck on his own for too long.'

Igor started to lurch away. After a few steps, however, he stopped and turned to face the girl.

'I'm sorry about what happened when we first met.' The words were almost a mumble because Igor wasn't used to apologizing. 'I hope I didn't frighten you too much.'

'That's all right, Igor,' Heinz Beans told him. 'I know you were only trying to help Fenella. Goodbye.'

Then Heinz Beans did something nobody had ever done to Igor before. She lifted up her hand and blew him a kiss. As he stumbled off into the night, tripping over the steps of the Dodgems, the warts on Igor's face were glowing with pleasure.

While she was waiting, Fenella wandered around the inside of the Ghost Train. Although Heinz Beans had explained that it was supposed to be frightening, Fenella really couldn't think why. One of her best friends was a ghost and she far preferred skeletons to most live human beings.

When she saw the cobwebs and model spiders, Fenella simply smiled. A friend of hers, Melissa Munch, used to breed spiders as pets. Real spiders, not pathetic little things like the models around her. The biggest of them was called Archie and Melissa used to ride around the castle on his back. In the end, though, Melissa had had to get rid of her pets. It had become such a nuisance having to use a sword to hack her way through the cobwebs when she wanted to move from one room to another. Besides, feeding them had also become a problem. Although Archie had been as gentle as a lamb with Melissa herself, he would insist on pouncing on visitors when they arrived at the castle. Poor Georgina Gulp had been wrapped in a silk cocoon and hung upside down in Archie's web for two nights before Melissa had realized her guest was missing.

Fenella was standing in front of a model which was wearing a black cloak and a tall, pointed hat when she heard the train start. The greenish skin, large, hooked nose and hairy chin all reminded her of somebody she knew, but she couldn't remember who. With Cousin Fred on his way, there were other things to think about and she stepped back into the shadows, a grim smile on her lips. She knew she would enjoy what was about to happen.

'Good girl,' Fred said approvingly to himself when the train suddenly stopped.

He assumed that his cousin was going to leave him there, where he was safe, until the terrible man had gone away. Then she would start the train again and bring him out.

Although most children would have hated to be stuck where he was, the Ghost Train didn't bother Fred at all. He had lived in the fair all his life and most of the things which made the younger kids squeal and scream were old friends to Fred. He had even given a lot of them names.

'There's old Sidney Spook,' he said to himself, ticking them off on his fingers, 'and Winnie the Witch and Boney the Skeleton and. . . . Hello, that's strange.'

Fred had noticed the figure deep in the shadows and he thought his father must have put in a new model without telling him. It was too dark for him to see much apart from the glowing eyes.

'They're jolly good, though,' he thought. 'That red colour is really scarey and they blink almost as if they're real.'

At that moment the figure began to move towards him, making Fred chuckle with delight. He knew there must be hidden wires pulling the model along.

'That's terrific,' he chortled. 'That should scare the pants off the customers all right. When they see this—'

And then Fred stopped because the model vampire didn't move as though it was being pulled by wires. Come to that, the closer the vampire approached, the less like a model it seemed. It looked like a vampire and it moved like a vampire and it smelled like a vampire and—

'Please,' Fred whispered, 'tell me you're not a vampire.'

'I can't do that,' Fenella hissed back. 'I was brought up not to tell lies.'

Fred would have liked to tell her she couldn't be a vampire, that they only existed in comics and films, but even he didn't believe this any longer. It was impossible when one of the creatures was there in front of him.

'Wh-wh-what d-d-do y-y-you w-w-want?' he stuttered.

'It's supper time,' Fenella replied with an awful smile. 'Guess who's on the menu tonight.'

'M-m-me?'

Fred pointed a shaking finger at himself.

'That's right, child. You should make a tasty snack.'

As she spoke, Fenella bared all her teeth and reached out for the terrified boy. Fred shrank back in his seat, sure that his last moment had come. He knew nothing could save him from the vampire. He tried to shout out for help but he was too frightened to make a sound.

At first, Fred couldn't understand why the vampire had suddenly stopped. It was only when she took a sudden step backwards that he noticed the dog standing beside the car. He hadn't heard Spot arrive but there he was. And, to Fred's amazement, the vampire seemed to be frightened of him.

'Get that thing away from me,' Fenella hissed. 'I can't abide dogs. Shoo, you nasty little beast.'

But Spot didn't shoo. Instead, he bounded forwards towards the vampire, yapping excitedly. Although he was wagging his tail, the puppy was making a lot of noise and the vampire appeared to be more frightened than ever.

'Call him off,' she cried.

Fred wouldn't have called him off even if he had been able to speak. Still barking, Spot jumped up at Fenella.

'Ow,' she yelled. 'The brute has bitten me.'

'Ow,' she yelled again as Spot jumped up once more.

Then the vampire turned and ran, chased by Spot. Fred didn't stop to see any more. As the vampire disappeared into the shadows in one direction Fred leaped from the car and began to run in the other, back to where he had seen his cousin. This was why he never knew that Fenella had stopped once she was out of sight. Laughing, she bent down to stroke the little dog.

'That was terrific, Spot,' she told him. 'You're a very clever dog.'

As a reward, she gave him two of the biscuits Igor had baked especially for the puppy. They were the reason Spot had been jumping up at Fenella and barking so excitedly. Like most puppies, Spot was very greedy.

'You stay here, Spot,' Fenella said as he settled down to eat. 'I'd better go and see how Heinz Beans is getting on.'

Silently, Fenella slipped back through the shadows until she was close enough to the entrance to overhear the children's voices. They were obviously talking about Igor.

'Are you sure he's gone?' Fred was asking nervously.

'Yes, he ran off the moment you went inside.'

'He must have been working for the vampire,' Fred said.

'What vampire? Are you imagining things?'

Heinz Beans was finding it difficult not to laugh.

'I'm not, honest. It was going to eat me until Spot drove it away. Come on. Let's get home quickly in case it comes back.'

'You go, Fred,' Heinz Beans told him. 'I'm not coming.'

'But you must. Mum and Dad have been worried sick and I've felt awful. I know it was all my fault. There won't be any more rotten tricks, I promise, especially after what you've done for me tonight.'

'I can't come back. I couldn't bear to lose Spot again.'

The puppy had just appeared at the entrance of the Ghost Train, licking his chops contentedly.

'Lose Spot!' Fred exclaimed, speaking as though he couldn't believe his ears. 'Lose the magnificent creature which saved my life! There's no way that's going to happen. I'll tell Mum and Dad what really happened before you ran away.'

'You'll get yourself into awful trouble.'

'I know,' Fred answered, 'but it's no more than I deserve for being so beastly to you and Spot. From now on I'm turning over a new leaf. I'm sure what happened tonight was some kind of punishment for me being so horrid.'

The girl was still hesitating and Fred reached

out to take hold of her arm.

'Please, Sara,' he said. 'Please come back. We've all missed you terribly.'

Inside the Ghost Train, Fenella was smiling to herself in the darkness as she turned away. She had heard enough to be sure things would work out all right. Perhaps Fred wasn't completely bad after all. *And* – her smile grew broader – she had at last found out what Heinz Beans's name really was.

Although she had enjoyed living with Fenella, it was nice to be in a real bed again in a real house. Sara snuggled down under the covers, careful not to disturb Spot who was asleep at the foot of the bed, and once again thought about what a marvellous night it had been. Aunt May and Uncle Albert had been so delighted to see her safe and sound that they hadn't been at all angry with her. Of course, Fred had helped a lot. He had been as good as his word and had explained how it was all his fault that she had run away. The best moment of all had been when she had spoken on the phone to Dad in Nigeria. Just talking to him had been wonderful but he had saved the most exciting news for the end of their conversation. Dad had arranged to fly back to England so he could spend a few days with her. The mere thought of seeing him again made her go tingly all over.

Tired as she was, she forced herself to keep her

eyes open. Everybody else had been in bed for over an hour and the house was quiet. She knew she wouldn't have long to wait. As soon as she heard the quiet tapping at the window, she scrambled out of bed to let Fenella in.

'How did it go?' Fenella asked.

'It was just like your Uncle Samuel said it would be. Please remember to thank him for me. Everybody was so pleased to see me, I felt mean about all the trouble I'd caused.'

'How about Fred?'

'He's been the nicest of all. I think he's really sorry for what he did.'

For a while they sat on the bed together and the girl explained everything that had happened. However, when she noticed how much her friend was yawning, Fenella decided it was time for her to go. The girl's face suddenly became sad, and she threw herself into Fenella's arms, hugging her tight.

'I shall miss you ever so much, Fenella,' she said.

'Don't be silly, child.' Fenella's own voice was rather gruff. 'Like I told you before, I'll come and visit whenever you want. Look. I have a going-away present for you.'

She reached into the folds of her shroud and brought something out. The girl curiously examined the small tube of metal.

'What is it?' she asked.

'You blow into it,' Fenella explained. 'It's a whistle.'

Although the girl did as Fenella had said, nothing happened. There was no sound at all.

'It doesn't work.'

'Oh yes it does,' Fenella laughed. 'You nearly deafened me. Come over to the window.'

When the girl looked out, she could see swarms of bats circling above the house. Higher up she thought she could see one or two larger shapes as well.

'It's a vampire whistle,' Fenella said. 'If you ever need me in a hurry, just blow the whistle and I'll be there before you know it.'

Fenella opened the window and, changing into her bat form, climbed on to the sill. Before she flew off, she turned back to look at the girl.

'There's one thing I've been meaning to ask you,' she said. 'I heard Fred call you Sara. Why didn't you tell me your real name before?'

'I'm sorry, Fenella.' Sara was feeling mean again. Although she hadn't actually lied about her name, she hadn't been honest with her friend either. 'At first I was afraid you might send me back if you knew my name. Then I got used to you calling me Heinz Beans.'

'I see.'

Fenella was silent for a few seconds.

'I always thought Heinz Beans was silly,' she said at last. 'I think Sara is much better.'

'So do I,' said Sara.

From the bed, Spot gave a sleepy little bark as though he agreed with them too.

Normally Fenella was pleased to return home, but tonight the crypt didn't seem the same. It felt empty without Sara and the puppy. Fenella herself was feeling sad and depressed.

'Snap out of it and stop feeling sorry for yourself,' she told herself sternly. 'Dracula's teeth, you've lived here for over three hundred years on your own. You should be used to it by now. Besides, there's lots for you to do.'

For a start, the crypt needed a good clean-out and it was high time the coffin was re-decorated. When she had the chance, she ought to fly over to Blood Castle and let Uncle Samuel know how his plan had worked. Then the bat-racing season would be starting soon and she would need to make herself some new outfits. It would never do to appear in last year's fashions.

There really were lots and lots of things for her to do but, deep down, Fenella wasn't fooling herself. She knew it would be a long, long time before she stopped missing the sight of Sara's smiling face when she climbed out of her coffin at night. There were occasions when being a vampire could be very lonely indeed.